against the wind
AN AGE GAP ROMANCE

TRISHA FUENTES

Against the Wind
An Age Gap Romance
Copyright © 2025 by Trisha Fuentes
All rights reserved.

Book Cover and formatting provided by Trisha Fuentes
https://bit.ly/m/trishafuentes

No part of this book may be reproduced in any form or by any electronic or mechanical means, including information storage and retrieval systems, without written permission from the author, except for the use of brief quotations in a book review.

ISBN: 979-8-3485-2990-1 (Paperback)

Published by
Ardent Artist Books
www.ardentartistbooks.com

about ardent artist books

➥ ABOUT US

Ardent Artist Books was established in 2008

We publish modern and historical romances once a month!

Get Your FREE List: Published & Upcoming Books
visit our website at:
https://bit.ly/3Wva4o0

* * *

➥ **WE HAVE BOOK TRAILERS TOO!**

Follow us on YouTube!
https://bit.ly/3W3xn7a

Like, Subscribe & Comment

* * *

➥ **READ SERIALIZED FICTION!**

Visit our website today to download one of our stories that unfold in bite-sized pieces!

Each installment is just 99¢!

https://bit.ly/3LsDpJL

* * *

➥ **LET'S CONNECT!**

Fuel your love of fiction with exclusive content and captivating insights from Ardent Artist Books. Whether you crave the thrill of modern narratives or the timeless elegance of historical fiction, our newsletter delivers a curated selection straight to your inbox. Plus, as a welcome gift, receive a FREE downloadable eBook:

"The Family Fix"
https://bit.ly/49BR3UB

contents

1. Seattle, Washington	1
2. The Gulfstream	9
3. The Alaskan Experience	25
4. Morning Revelations	41
5. The Snowstorm	55
6. Stay The Night	67
7. Missed Calls	77
8. We Need Food	89
9. A Small Gathering	101
10. Half-Truths	111
11. Soft Blankets	121
12. Saved By A Tractor	133
13. Love or Lust?	143
14. A Fool Who Fell Too Hard	153
15. Play The Game	163
About Trisha	177
Also by Trisha Fuentes	179

CHAPTER ONE

seattle, washington

NORA KRAMER

I ADJUST my navy blazer in Sea-Tac's private aviation terminal, watching dawn spill across the tarmac like honey. At forty-three, I've earned every gold stripe on my sleeve, each one a chapter in my twenty-year love affair with the sky. The morning light catches in my auburn hair as I study my reflection in the wall of windows, noting the subtle laugh lines that speak more of experience than age.

The Gulfstream G650 waits outside, its aluminum skin transformed to liquid silver in the morning light. I love these charter flights into Alaska's remote corners—they feel like threading a needle between worlds, braiding the polished luxury of executive aviation with the raw necessity of frontier life.

My heels tap against the terminal floor as I complete my pre-flight routine, each step precise and deliberate. The familiar scent of jet fuel drifts through the air conditioning, and I breathe it in like others might savor their morning coffee. It still thrills me, even after all these years.

Flying has been in my blood since before I could walk. My earliest memories are of sitting on Dad's shoulders at Andrews Air Force Base, pointing at F-15s streaking across the Maryland sky while he taught me their call signs. I'd stretch my arms out like wings, imagining the freedom of soaring through clouds, defying gravity with nothing but skill and engineering.

"That'll be you one day, kiddo," Dad would say, his voice full of pride even then.

I trace my fingers along my captain's stripes, remembering the countless hours spent poring over physics textbooks and flight manuals. While other girls in my high school decorated their lockers with boy band posters, mine displayed diagrams of lift coefficients and wing designs. My guidance counselor raised her eyebrows when I loaded up on advanced math and sciences, but I knew exactly what I needed.

"You should consider the Air Force Academy," Dad suggested during my senior year, his own service medals gleaming from their display case in our living room. The possibility tugged at me – following his footsteps, serving my country, flying those same jets that had captured my imagination.

But something else called to me. The freedom of civilian aviation, the chance to chart my own course. I still remember his face when I told him I was going for my private pilot's license instead. Not disappointment – understanding.

"The sky's still the sky, no matter what uniform you wear," he said, hugging me tight.

Sarah, my co-pilot of three years, meets me for the external inspection. We move around the aircraft in practiced synchronization, like dancers who've memorized the steps.

"Clear skies to Anchorage," she says, clipboard catching the light. "Should be smooth sailing."

I run my fingers along the Gulfstream's fuselage, another habit inherited from Dad. He taught me to read planes like stories, their metal skin holding tales of turbulence and triumph. Twenty years in the cockpit, and still that first touch sends electricity through my fingertips.

The Rolls-Royce engines purr to life with their familiar expensive whisper. I feel the vibration in my bones as we lift into the morning sky, Seattle's urban geometry falling away beneath us like a discarded puzzle. At cruise altitude, the horizon curves away in an infinite embrace, clouds below us sculpted into canyons and peaks by invisible hands.

The first warning light appears three hours in, a tiny red star born on my instrument panel.

"Sarah." I keep my voice level, though my pulse picks up tempo. "You seeing this?"

"Port engine readings are off." Her hands move across the panels with surgical precision. "Pressure's fluctuating."

The vibration starts as a whisper, a secret the plane doesn't want to tell. Our eight passengers—a mix of weathered engineers bound for Anchorage's latest pipeline project and grandparents with eyes bright at the thought of first hugs with grandchildren—won't notice, but I feel it like a fever in the airframe. The sky around us suddenly seems vast and empty, the distance to safety stretching like taffy.

"Where's the nearest airport?" I ask, voice secure.

Sarah looks down at her phone, "Wrangell."

"Wrangell, ever been?" I ask, curious.

"Once, a year ago, cute town," Sarah says, adjusting the buttons on her uniform.

"Seattle Center, Alpine Charter 2187." My voice remains steady as a heartbeat. "Requesting immediate diversion to Wrangell. We're showing engine irregularities."

The next hour unspools like a wire under tension. I nurse the failing engine, coaxing the Gulfstream through the sky like a wounded bird. Each minute feels stretched and fragile as spun glass. When Wrangell's runway finally emerges from the clouds—a strip of civilization carved from the Alaskan wilderness—my hands are steady but my spine thrums with electricity.

The landing hits harder than I'd like, *but any landing you can walk away from is a good one*—Dad's words echoing in my head like a mantra. The port engine gives one final shudder as we taxi to a stop, like a tired animal laying down to rest.

Only after the last passenger has deplaned do I allow myself to feel the tremors in my hands, adrenaline leaving my system like tidewater draining from a harbor.

Through the tiny terminal's windows, I watch maintenance crews swarm my wounded aircraft.

"Could be here a while." Sarah appears at my elbow with coffee that smells like it's been brewing since statehood. "That part's not exactly standard inventory in Wrangell."

My mind spins through contingencies like a roulette wheel, each option less appealing than the last. Our charter service prides itself on reliability—delays ripple through schedules like stones thrown in still water.

"There might be another option." Sarah's voice drops low, conspiratorial. "There's this mechanic in town. Bit of a legend among the bush pilots. They say he can fix anything with wings, manual or no manual."

The wilderness stretches beyond the windows like an abstract painting in shades of green and gray. I feel possibility tickle the back of my neck—or maybe it's just Alaska's winter breath sneaking through the terminal's aging weather stripping.

My phone feels heavy as a stone as I pull it from my pocket, Dad's voice surfacing from memory: "The sky forgives no mistakes, but it rewards creative thinking." The mechanic's number appears on my screen like a riddle waiting to be solved.

The phone rings once, twice. When the deep voice answers, I feel something shift in the air around me, like a weather front moving in—the kind that changes landscapes and rewrites futures. I don't know it yet, but this unscheduled landing will turn out to be the most important mistake I've ever made.

CHAPTER TWO
the gulfstream
BEN HUFFMAN

THE SYMPHONY of pneumatic tools and the percussion of metal on metal filled my ears when I heard Jace calling my name. I slid out from under the ancient Cessna, grease mapping constellations across my calloused hands and—if experience is any teacher—probably streaked like war paint across my face too.

"Hey boss." Jace leaned against the hangar door, winter light haloing his silhouette, phone held like a winning lottery ticket. "Got something interesting for you. Gulfstream G650 grounded over at Wrangell Airport. They're asking for you specifically."

Something electric ran through my spine at the words. A G650—that's corporate money, *old money*, the kind of aircraft that usually has manufacturer's mechanics flown in from Seattle or Anchorage at the first hint of trouble. My world is bush planes and float planes, the workhorses of Alaska's endless twilight.

"A Gulfstream?" I pushed myself to my feet, joints popping like cheap fireworks. At twenty-eight, I'm not that old, but a decade and a half of crawling around hangars leaves its signature on a man's body. "That's new. Who's the operator?"

"Alpine Charter Services. Their captain's some hotshot from Seattle. Sarah Monroe—you remember her? The bush pilot who saved that family last winter?—she's the one who gave them your name."

My reputation is a strange currency in Alaska. I can coax ancient engines back to life and diagnose electrical gremlins by touch, but luxury jets? They're a different breed entirely. Still, an aircraft in trouble is an aircraft in trouble, and I've never been one to turn away a challenge.

I glanced at the Cessna, its exposed engine a familiar puzzle of steel and aluminum. The Gulfstream will be all digital diagnostics and composite materials, a testament to how far aviation has come from the bush pilot days. But underneath all that polish and sophistication, it's still just a machine trying to defy gravity.

"Tell them I'm on my way." I reached for my jacket, the leather worn smooth as river stones at the elbows. "And Jace? Get the hangar ready. Something tells me this isn't going to be a simple fix."

Jace tosses me a fresh rag. "Might want to clean up first though. Looking a bit rough around the edges."

I glance at my reflection in a nearby window. Sure enough, there's a black streak across my forehead. "Could be worse."

"Could be better too." Diego, my other mechanic, pipes up from across the hangar. "First impressions."

"Since when do you care about first impressions?" I call back while gathering my tools.

"Since never. But you're representing all of us grease monkeys now."

They're not wrong. A commercial job could mean good things for the shop. I head to the small bathroom and do my best to look presentable, though 'presentable' in my line of work is relative.

My mind drifts back to my first "repair job" - Dad's old snowblower when I was twelve. The spark plug was shot, but I was convinced I could fix it. Spent three hours in our garage in Palmer, tools scattered everywhere, until that engine finally turned over. The pride in Dad's eyes that day set me on this path.

"You've got the touch, son," he'd said, his calloused hand squeezing my shoulder. Those words echoed through every repair job after - from lawnmowers to ATVs, then to cars in high school. While other kids were playing video games, I was elbow-deep in engines, learning their language of pistons and valves.

The first airplane I worked on was Mr. Peterson's bush plane, a temperamental Piper SuperCub that no one else could figure out. I was nineteen, fresh out of A&P school, and terrified of screwing up. But machines have always made sense to me in a way people sometimes don't. Their problems have solutions - concrete, logical fixes. You just have to listen to what they're telling you.

A massive cargo plane roars overhead as I take the airport exit. Even after all these years, I still look up every time. There's something magical about these metal giants that never gets old. Dad understood that. He was the one who pushed me to specialize in aircraft maintenance when I was waffling between careers.

"Cars are fine," he'd said, "but planes? That's where the real challenge is. When a car breaks down, you pull over.

When a plane breaks down..." He didn't need to finish that sentence.

The shop came later, after years of working for others and saving every penny. Dad helped me secure the loan, cosigned without hesitation. "Alaska needs good mechanics," he'd insisted. "Especially up here where flying isn't a luxury - it's a lifeline."

He was right. In five years, I've built a reputation that brings in work from all over the state. Bush pilots trust me with their lives - *literally*. Every repair has to be perfect because there's no roadside assistance at 10,000 feet.

I pull into the airport's maintenance area, flashing my credentials at the security gate. The commercial terminal looms ahead, gleaming in the morning sun. This isn't my usual territory - I'm more comfortable in my own hangar with its familiar smells of oil and metal - but a problem is a problem, no matter how big the aircraft.

A ground crew member waves me toward Hangar C. Through the massive doors, I can see the silhouette of what looks like an Airbus. My tool bag feels heavier suddenly. This is definitely not my usual bush plane territory, but the principles are the same. Hydraulics are hydraulics, whether they're on a Super Cub or a commercial airliner.

The hangar echoes with activity as I park. Maintenance crews scurry around like ants, their orange vests bright against the concrete floor. Someone's called out "The specialist is here!" and heads turn my way. I grab my bag and step out into the controlled chaos, already running through hydraulic systems in my mind.

A woman in a pilot's uniform strides toward me, her expression a mix of concern and barely contained frustration. Her posture screams authority, but there's something else there too - a kind of intensity that catches me off guard. She's not what I expected, and for a moment, I forget every single thing I know about aircraft mechanics.

I shift my tool bag to my left hand and clear my throat. Time to focus. This is just another puzzle to solve, even if it comes with an unexpectedly distracting pilot attached to it.

I can tell the woman's not happy about needing outside help. Her posture screams authority and competence, making me suddenly aware of every wrinkle in my coveralls.

As I approach, toolbox in hand, her eyes narrow slightly. I've seen that look before - the one that says I'm too young to know what I'm doing. At twenty-eight, I'm used to it.

"Ms. Kramer?" I extend my hand. "Ben Huffman."

She takes it with professional courtesy, but her handshake is brief. "You're the specialist Thompson recommended?"

"That's me. Mind if I take a look?"

Her lips press into a thin line. "Our maintenance crew has already conducted thorough inspections."

"And I'm sure they're excellent at their jobs." I keep my tone light, casual. "But sometimes a fresh set of eyes helps. Different perspective and all that."

She studies me for a moment longer before nodding curtly. "The issue appears to be in the hydraulic system. We're getting irregular pressure readings in the landing gear."

I set down my toolbox and pull out my tablet. "Can I see the maintenance logs?"

She produces them immediately, and I notice her watching intently as I scroll through the data. The readings are definitely odd - not a standard pattern I've seen before.

"Mind if I check the undercarriage?"

"Be my guest." Her tone suggests she's not expecting much.

I get to work, methodically examining the components while explaining what I'm looking for. Most clients prefer silence, but something tells me Ms. Kramer appreciates information.

"See this connection here?" I point to a seemingly innocent joint. "The wear pattern's unusual. Might indicate..."

"A micro-fracture in the adjacent line?" she finishes, stepping closer to see where I'm pointing.

I glance up, surprised and impressed. "Exactly. Most pilots don't catch that kind of detail."

"Most pilots haven't been flying for twenty years." But there's less edge in her voice now.

The Alaskan wind whips around us as I continue my inspection, carrying the scent of pine and snow from the distant mountains. Behind us, ground crew members hustle across the tarmac, their voices carrying in the clear air. It's a stark contrast to the urban jungle I know she's used to - out here, nature's always reminding you who's really in charge.

A group of locals passes by, dressed in their typical mix of practical layers and winter gear, offering friendly waves. Ms. Kramer returns them automatically, but I catch her slight bewilderment at their casual familiarity.

"Welcome to Alaska," I grin. "Where everyone's a neighbor, even if they live fifty miles away."

She doesn't smile back, but her shoulders relax slightly. "How long until you can give me an assessment?"

I stand, brushing off my knees. "I've got good news and bad news. The good news is, I know what's wrong. Bad news..." I brace for her reaction, "You're looking at at least a forty-eight-hour repair window."

Her jaw tightens, but she maintains her composure. "That's not acceptable. There must be a way to expedite the process."

"I understand the position this puts you in." And I do - I've worked with enough pilots to know what delays mean for their schedules, their passengers, their careers. "But this isn't something we can rush. Not if we want to ensure everyone's safety."

For a moment, we stand in silence, the wind tugging at her perfectly arranged hair while she processes this information.

I can't help but stare at her as she processes the news, struck by how she holds herself together despite the obvious setback. Most pilots I deal with would be cursing up a storm by now, but Ms. Kramer maintains this quiet dignity that's somehow more compelling than any outburst.

The wind plays with strands of her dark hair, and I notice flecks of silver at her temples that catch the sunlight. There's something magnetic about the way she carries herself - a natural authority that comes from years of commanding aircraft and crew. Her uniform fits her perfectly, the crisp lines emphasizing her confident posture.

"Mr. Huffman," she says, catching me watching her. I quickly avert my eyes, focusing on my tablet instead. "Is there any possibility at all—"

"Ben," I interrupt, then immediately regret my informality. "Sorry, I mean... everyone just calls me Ben."

A slight pause. I risk looking up and catch an expression I can't quite read crossing her face. For a split second, she seems thrown off balance - not by the situation, but by *me*. Her eyes meet mine, and there's this moment of... something. Recognition? Interest?

I clear my throat. "The thing is, Ms. Kramer, even if I pulled an all-nighter, which I'm willing to do, we're still looking at a mandatory testing period. FAA regulations are pretty strict about—"

"I'm familiar with the regulations." Her voice has a slight edge, but it's not unkind. She steps closer to look at my tablet, and I catch a hint of her perfume - something subtle and expensive that makes my heart rate kick up a notch.

"Right, of course you are." I'm usually more articulate than this. Something about her proximity is scrambling my brain circuits. "I just meant..."

"Show me exactly what you're seeing." She leans in closer, her shoulder nearly touching mine as she studies the diagnostic readings. I try to focus on the numbers, but I'm acutely aware of her presence, the professional way she carries herself somehow making her even more attractive.

I point to several data points, explaining the pattern I've noticed. She asks sharp, intelligent questions that reveal a deeper technical knowledge than most pilots possess. Each question makes me more intrigued. It's rare to find someone who can keep up with the technical aspects of what I do, let alone challenge my thinking.

"That's... actually a good observation," she admits, sounding surprised at her own concession. When I glance at her, there's a hint of color in her cheeks that wasn't there before. She takes a step back, creating distance between us, and I wonder if she felt it too - that spark of connection that has nothing to do with aircraft mechanics.

"I try my best," I say, attempting to keep my tone light despite the sudden tension in the air. "Listen, I know this isn't ideal, but I promise you I'll make this my top priority. Whatever it takes to get you back in the air safely."

She's studying me now, her expression guarded but curious. I feel exposed under her gaze, like she's running through her own diagnostic checks. My hands itch to keep busy, to grab a wrench or check another component - anything to distract from this charged moment.

"You have a reputation for being the best," she says finally. "Thompson wouldn't stop talking about you. I thought he was exaggerating."

"Was?"

"I'm reserving judgment until I see results." But there's a slight upturn at the corner of her mouth that makes my pulse jump. "Though your initial assessment seems... thorough."

I should be focusing on the hydraulic system. I should be planning out the repair sequence or calling my shop to rearrange my schedule. Instead, I'm noticing how her eyes crinkle slightly at the corners when she's thinking, how she absentmindedly touches the pilot's wings pinned to her uniform when she's processing information.

A ground crew member calls out to her, breaking the moment. She straightens, professional mask firmly back in place. "I need to make some calls, arrange accommodations—"

"The Moose Haven," I quickly say, watching her eyebrows raise. "A Bed and Breakfast here in town."

She glances at me. "You'll keep me updated on your progress?"

"Absolutely. Every step." I pull out my business card, suddenly self-conscious of the grease stain on one corner. "My direct line. Call anytime."

She takes the card, her fingers brushing mine briefly. That

small contact shouldn't feel as electric as it does. "Anytime?"

"Day or night. I mean, you know, for updates about the plane." *I'm usually smoother than this. What is wrong with me?*

"Of course." Is she fighting back a smile? "For the plane."

I watch her walk away, her confident stride carrying her across the hangar floor. Just before she reaches the door, she glances back over her shoulder, catching me staring again. This time, I don't look away quite fast enough, and I swear I see a flicker of something in her expression - surprise, maybe even pleasure - before she disappears through the door.

I exhale slowly, trying to get my head back in the game. I've got forty-eight hours of intense work ahead of me, and I need to focus on hydraulics and pressure systems, not the way Ms. Kramer's presence seems to have thrown my own internal systems completely off balance.

The repair itself is complex enough to demand my full attention. But as I start laying out my tools and planning my approach, I keep thinking about that moment when our eyes met, the subtle shift in her composure when I caught her off guard. The way she tried to maintain professional distance even as something pulled us into each other's orbit.

A maintenance crew member approaches with some paperwork, and I force myself to concentrate on the task at hand. But part of my mind is already wondering when she'll call for that first update, and what excuse I can find to see her in person instead of just giving it over the phone.

CHAPTER THREE
the alaskan experience
NORA KRAMER

THE MOOSE HAVEN INN rises before me like a testament to Alaskan perseverance – a three-story Victorian masterpiece in weathered blue-gray clapboard with crisp white trim that's seen at least a century of harsh winters. Through the wraparound porch's delicate latticework, I spot a cluster of rocking chairs facing the distant peaks of the Wrangell Mountains. Inside, the renovation work is evident in the seamless blend of original features – exposed wooden beams, a grand staircase with intricate spindles, and stone fireplaces – with modern amenities like updated lighting and plush furniture.

The aroma of fresh-baked bread and coffee wafts from the kitchen, mixing with the scent of pine from massive flower arrangements.

I recognize the Hendersons settling into the cozy library nook, and the Martinez family exploring the sunny breakfast room with its wall of windows. The engineers, who'd been so understanding about the delay, are examining historic black and white photographs in the foyer while Thomas Chen, my loyal flyer, unpacks his briefcase in the parlor, apparently planning to make the best of this unexpected layover by catching up on paperwork. Mrs. Patterson, my most vocal critic during the delay announcement, stands at the front desk, probably lodging another complaint about circumstances beyond anyone's control. But even her sour mood can't diminish the warmth of this place, with its hand-sewn quilts draped over leather armchairs, local artworks adorning every wall, and the distinct feeling that I've somehow stumbled into someone's well-loved home rather than a commercial establishment.

I pace across the hotel room, checking my phone for the hundredth time. Still no update from maintenance. My footsteps echo against the thin carpet as I move from window to desk to door and back again. The small digital clock on the nightstand seems to mock me with each passing minute.

"Yes, I understand the implications." I grip the phone tighter during the call with my supervisor. "No, I can't give you an exact timeline yet. The mechanic is still—" A sigh escapes before I can catch it. "Of course, I'll keep you updated."

Ending the call, I press my forehead against the cool window glass. From here, I can see the hangar where my plane sits, Ben's figure moving purposefully around it. Even from this distance, there's something magnetic about his presence. The thought catches me off guard.

My reflection stares back at me, and I notice the slight flush in my cheeks. *What is wrong with me?* I'm acting like some lovesick teenager, not a seasoned pilot with fifteen years of experience. But there's something about the way he moves, the confidence in his hands as they work over the engine, the easy smile that seems permanently etched on his face...

I flip through the maintenance reports for the tenth time, but the words blur together. My mind keeps drifting back to earlier today, to that first moment Ben walked up to my plane. The memory hits me with unexpected force.

He'd emerged from his truck with such casual confidence, toolbox in one hand, coffee in the other. My initial irritation at his apparent youth melted away when those startling blue eyes met mine. Dark hair fell across his forehead in a way that seemed deliberately casual, yet

I doubted he spent more than two seconds thinking about it.

"Get it together, Kramer," I mutter to myself, pushing away from the desk. But the image persists – the way his hands moved over the engine components with such surety, the slight quirk of his lips when he explained the mechanical issue. Each detail burns in my memory with embarrassing clarity.

My heart had actually fluttered. *Fluttered*. Like I was some romance novel heroine instead of a professional pilot with decades of experience. The worst part? It still does a little jump when I think about him. About the way his forearms looked with his sleeves rolled up, the quiet competence in his movements.

I press my palms against my eyes. "This is ridiculous." The words echo in the empty hotel room. He can't be more than thirty – definitely closer to twenty-five than thirty-five. The math makes me groan. When I was starting flight school, he was probably still playing with toy planes.

Walking to the bathroom, I stare hard at my reflection. Sure, I take care of myself. Regular exercise, good skincare routine, healthy diet. But there's no denying the subtle signs of age – fine lines at the corners of my eyes, the slight softening along my jaw. *What would someone like Ben want with a woman my age?*

Not that it matters. Not that I should even be thinking about it. I'm stranded here because of a mechanical issue, not to indulge in some inappropriate fantasy about a mechanic who's young enough to... I can't even finish the thought.

But then I remember how he looked at me when explaining the repair process. There was respect there, genuine professional admiration. And something else? Or am I just seeing what I want to see, letting my imagination run wild because I'm stuck in this remote town with nothing else to focus on?

The memory of his laugh catches me off guard – rich and genuine when I'd made a dry comment about Alaska's weather. The way his eyes crinkled at the corners, how the sound seemed to warm something inside me that I hadn't even realized was cold.

"This is unprofessional," I tell my reflection firmly. But the woman in the mirror looks flushed, alive in a way I haven't felt in years. The pilot's uniform I'm still wearing feels suddenly constraining, and I tug at the collar.

Turning away from the mirror, I try to focus on the practicalities. The flight schedule, the passengers who need to be rebooked, the reports I need to file. But my thoughts keep circling back to him like a compass finding true north. The gentle confidence in his voice when he assured me he could fix the issue. The way his t-shirt stretched across his shoulders as he leaned over the engine.

A text notification breaks through my reverie. My heart jumps before I can stop it, but it's just the airline updating me on passenger arrangements. The disappointment I feel is both immediate and mortifying. *What am I doing, hoping for a message from him? What would I even say if he did contact me?*

I sink onto the edge of the bed, letting out a long breath. The isolation of this small Alaskan town suddenly feels dangerous. Like being removed from my normal life has created this bubble where impossible things seem possible. Where the age gap between Ben and me doesn't seem like an insurmountable obstacle.

But it is. It has to be. I've built my career on being professional, on making smart decisions. On never letting emotion cloud my judgment. And yet here I am, acting like a teenager with her first crush. The worst part is, I can't seem to stop. Every time I push thoughts of him away, they come flooding back stronger than before.

His hands. His eyes. The way he moves with such unselfconscious grace. The quiet intelligence behind his casual demeanor. Each detail feels branded into my memory, refusing to fade no matter how much I tell myself to focus on something else.

"What is wrong with me?" I whisper to the empty room. The question hangs in the air, unanswered. *Because how do I explain this? How do I rationalize feeling this way about someone so much younger? Someone who probably sees me as nothing more than another client, another pilot with a broken plane?*

"Get it together, Kramer," I mutter to myself. I've dealt with countless mechanics over my career. None of them have made my stomach flip like this. None of them have been young enough to make me feel like a predatory cougar either.

The knock at my door nearly makes me jump out of my skin.

"Ms. Kramer?" Ben's voice carries through the door. "Got a minute?"

My heart races as I smooth down my hair. This is ridiculous. I'm a professional. Taking a deep breath, I open the door.

Ben stands there, still in his work clothes, that infectious smile lighting up his face. "Thought I saw you watching from up here."

Heat floods my cheeks. "I was just checking on the progress."

"Right." His eyes twinkle with amusement. "Look, I know this isn't ideal for you, being stuck here."

"That's an understatement."

"Thing is, I've been there. Got stranded in Juneau once for three days during a snowstorm. Nearly went crazy staring at hotel walls." He leans against the doorframe, casual as can be. "Let me show you around town. Better than wearing a path in that carpet."

My first instinct is to refuse. Being alone with him seems dangerous in ways I can't quite articulate. "I should really stay close to monitor the repairs..."

"The repairs will happen whether you're watching or not. Come on, when's the last time you actually explored one of the places you fly to?"

There's something disarming about his earnestness that makes my usual defenses waver. "I... I don't know if that's appropriate."

"It's just lunch and a tour. Nothing inappropriate about that." He pushes off the doorframe. "Unless you want it to be."

The comment sends a jolt through me, but his expression remains innocent. "I suppose some fresh air might help."

"That's the spirit!" His enthusiasm is contagious. "There's this great little cafe downtown. Best salmon chowder you'll ever taste."

Twenty minutes later, we're walking down the main street of the small town. The transition from airport to downtown took all of five minutes – a far cry from the urban sprawl I'm used to.

"So this is downtown?" I can't keep the skepticism from my voice.

"Hey, don't knock it till you've tried it. We might not have skyscrapers, but we've got character."

He's not wrong. The buildings are a charming mix of historic and practical, with hanging flower baskets adding splashes of color to the wooden storefronts. Mountain peaks loom in the background, making the town feel nestled and protected.

"That's the original trading post," Ben points out as we pass a weathered building. "Built in 1912. Story goes, the founder won it in a poker game from a Russian fur trader."

Despite myself, I find my lips curving into a smile. "You're making that up."

"Cross my heart." He grins back at me. "I've got more where that came from. Wait till you hear about the great moose uprising of 1947."

"Now I know you're lying."

His laugh is warm and genuine, and I feel something inside me starting to unwind. The constant tension in my shoulders begins to ease as we make our way to the cafe, his stories becoming more outlandish with each block.

For the first time since the mechanical issue grounded us, I find myself thinking that maybe, just maybe, this delay isn't the worst thing that could have happened.

The cafe appears ahead, a cozy building with large windows and a hand-painted sign. The smell of fresh bread and coffee wafts out as Ben holds the door open for me. Our fingers brush as I pass him, and the contact sends an electric current straight through me.

I'm in trouble. Real trouble.

I try to focus on the menu, but my eyes keep drifting to Ben's hands as he points out his favorite dishes. His fingers are long, elegant despite the engine grease still lingering under his nails. I imagine those hands sliding across my skin, and heat floods my face.

"The chowder's amazing, but honestly?" His thumb traces the edge of his water glass. "Their sourdough bread is what keeps me coming back. They've had the same starter going for thirty years."

I nod, not trusting my voice. My gaze catches on the strong line of his throat as he takes a drink, watching the movement of his Adam's apple. The casual grace of him is mesmerizing. A drop of water clings to his lower lip, and I have to grip my menu tighter to keep from reaching across the table to brush it away.

"Ms. Kramer? You still with me?"

I snap my attention back to his eyes, mortified at being caught staring. "Sorry, I was just... thinking about the mechanical issues."

"Right." His smile suggests he doesn't believe me for a second. "The mechanical issues. That's why you're blushing?"

"I don't blush." The protest comes out weaker than intended.

"No? Must be the lighting then." He leans forward, lowering his voice. "Though I gotta say, it's a good look on you."

My heart hammers against my ribs. I've never experienced anything like this before – this raw, immediate attraction that bypasses all my carefully constructed walls. Every movement he makes draws my attention like a magnet. The way his lips form words, how his shoulders shift under his shirt, the casual confidence in his posture.

"You're very... direct." I manage to keep my voice steady, professional.

"Life's too short not to be." His eyes meet mine, and there's heat there that makes my breath catch. "Especially when something – or someone – interests you."

I've built my career on control, on never letting emotions interfere with judgment. But watching his mouth curve into that knowing smile, all I can think about is how those lips would feel against mine. *Would he be gentle? Or would there be an edge of hunger to match the look in his eyes?*

"The salmon here..." He's still talking, explaining something about local fishing, but I'm lost in watching his mouth move. The flash of white teeth, the way his tongue darts out to wet his lips. I've never been this distracted by someone's physical presence before. Never felt this visceral pull toward another person.

"You're doing it again." His voice holds a note of amused satisfaction.

"Doing what?"

"Staring at my mouth instead of listening to me." He traces the rim of his glass again, deliberately this time. "Should I be flattered?"

Heat crawls up my neck. "I was not—"

"You were. Are." His grin widens. "Don't worry, I don't mind. Especially since I've been trying not to stare at you since we met."

"That's..." I swallow hard. "That's very inappropriate."

"Probably." He shrugs, unrepentant. "But true. You've got this presence about you – commanding but elegant. Like a queen who somehow ended up in my little corner of Alaska."

The compliment shouldn't affect me this much. I've heard worse lines delivered with more polish. But there's something genuine in his tone that gets under my skin, makes me feel seen in a way I haven't in years.

"You can't just say things like that." But I'm smiling despite myself.

"Why not? Because I'm younger? Because we're working together?" He leans back, studying me. "Or because it makes you think about things you shouldn't?"

My mouth goes dry. "Both. All of it."

"Age is just a number." His foot brushes mine under the table, and I know it's not accidental. "And this job won't last forever. As for thinking about things you shouldn't..." His eyes drop to my breasts before meeting mine again. "Maybe those are exactly the things you should be thinking about."

I should shut this down. Should establish clear professional boundaries. Instead, I find myself playing with my napkin, pulse racing. "And what things do you think I'm thinking about?"

"Same things I am, probably." His voice drops lower, sending shivers down my spine. "Like how your hair would feel between my fingers. Whether you taste as elegant as you look."

"Ben..." It comes out somewhere between a warning and a plea.

"Tell me you don't want to know." He challenges softly. "Tell me you haven't wondered what my hands would feel like on your skin."

I can't tell him that, because God help me, I *have* wondered. Have been wondering since he first walked up to my plane. The attraction is physical, primal in a way I've never experienced. Every nerve ending in my body seems attuned to his presence.

"This is dangerous." But I don't move away when his fingers brush mine on the table.

"The best things usually are." His thumb traces circles on my wrist, and the simple touch sends electricity through my entire body. "You feel it too, don't you? This... pull."

"Yes." The admission comes out barely above a whisper. "But that doesn't make it right."

"Doesn't make it wrong either." His eyes hold mine, intense and unflinching. "Sometimes the best things in life come from taking chances."

The waitress approaches with our food, and Ben withdraws his hand. The loss of contact leaves my skin tingling, aching for more. I've never believed in instant attraction, in chemistry so strong it overwhelms reason. But sitting here, watching Ben's hands wrap around his coffee mug, all I can think about is how those fingers would feel tangled in my hair, tracing the curve of my spine.

"Try the chowder." His voice has returned to normal volume, but there's still heat in his eyes. "Trust me."

Trust. Such a simple word for such a complicated situation. But as I lift the spoon to my lips, feeling his gaze follow the movement, I realize I might already be past the point of choosing whether or not to trust him. Past the point of choosing anything rational at all.

CHAPTER FOUR
morning revelations
NORA KRAMER

SUNLIGHT STREAMS through the thin hotel curtains, and for the first time since being grounded here, I wake up without that knot of anxiety in my stomach. Instead, there's a flutter of... anticipation? The thought of seeing Ben at the hangar today brings an involuntary smile to my face.

I catch my reflection in the mirror and shake my head. "Get it together, Nora." What am I doing, getting excited about seeing a mechanic who's barely older than my nephew?

The hotel's complimentary breakfast is busier than usual. As I pour myself a cup of coffee, Diana, one of the servers I've gotten to know over the past few days, slides a fresh plate of pastries onto the buffet.

"Good morning, Captain Kramer! Saw you yesterday with that handsome young mechanic." She winks. "He's quite popular around here – always helping people out when their cars break down or their heaters go on the fritz."

Heat creeps up my neck. "He's just working on my plane."

"Mmhmm." Diana's knowing smile makes me feel like a teenager. "Well, he's a good one. Not like those fly-by-night contractors who come through here."

I busy myself with selecting a bagel, but can't help asking, "Known him long?"

"Since he was fifteen. Fixed my grandson's bike last summer, wouldn't take a dime for it." She adjusts her apron. "Never seen him spend so much time showing anyone around town though."

I clear my throat, desperate to change the subject. "The coffee's especially good today."

"Sure is." She gives me another wink before moving to greet new guests.

The dining room's large windows offer a view of the small town's main street. Unlike my first day here when everything seemed depressingly provincial, I now notice charming details – the hand-painted signs, the way everyone greets each other by name, the mountains framing every view. The place has a pulse, a rhythm all its own.

Thinking I'll grab a coffee to go before heading to the hangar, I walk the short distance to The Daily Grind, the café Ben recommended yesterday. The bell chimes as I push open the door, and there he is, sitting at the counter with a half-eaten breakfast in front of him.

"Nora!" His face lights up, and my heart does something entirely unprofessional. "Great minds think alike."

"Morning." I try to sound casual as I slide onto the stool next to him. "Didn't expect to see you here."

"Best breakfast in town." He pushes his plate aside, turning to face me. "Try the sourdough pancakes – they're life-changing."

"Just coffee for me."

"Come on, live a little." His eyes crinkle at the corners when he smiles. "I'll split an order with you."

Before I can protest, he's already signaling the waitress. "Hey June, can we get some of those famous pancakes? And coffee for the captain here."

"You don't have to—"

"I want to." His knee bumps mine under the counter, and neither of us moves away. "Besides, you can't properly judge a town until you've tried its signature breakfast."

The pancakes arrive, golden and steaming. Ben's right – they're incredible, tangy, and light with a crispy edge. We fall into easy conversation about our morning routines, and I find myself telling him about my first solo flight.

"Fifteen years of flying, and I still get that rush during takeoff." I trace the rim of my coffee cup. "Like anything's possible."

"That's how I feel when I solve a particularly tricky mechanical issue." Ben's enthusiasm is contagious. "There's this moment when everything clicks into place..."

"And you know you've got it," we finish together, then laugh at the synchronicity.

The morning light streams through the café windows, catching the gold flecks in his hazel eyes. He's younger, yes, but there's a depth to him that catches me off guard. His hands, strong and capable from years of mechanical work, gesture expressively as he tells me about his apprenticeship.

"Most guys thought I was crazy, starting so young," he admits. "But I knew exactly what I wanted to do."

"That kind of certainty is rare." I find myself leaning closer. "I respect that."

He holds my gaze a moment too long, and the air between us shifts, charges with something I'm not ready to name. The café's wall clock chimes nine, breaking the spell.

"I should head to the hangar." Ben pulls out his wallet despite my protests. "Need to check on those replacement parts."

"I'll walk with you." The words come out before I can stop them. "Need to file some paperwork anyway."

Outside, the morning is crisp and clear. We fall into step together, our shoulders occasionally brushing. The small-town streets are coming alive, and several people call out greetings to Ben. He knows them all by name, asking after family members and sharing quick jokes.

I watch him interact with his community, seeing how deeply rooted he is here despite his youth. There's something attractive about that stability, that sense of belonging. It's so different from my life of constant movement, of cities blurring together in an endless stream.

"What are you thinking about?" Ben asks softly.

I start to deflect with something casual about the weather, but his genuine interest makes me honest. "Just... how different our lives are. You've built something real here."

"Different doesn't mean incompatible." His voice is careful, measured. "Sometimes the best combinations are unexpected ones."

The loaded silence that follows makes my pulse quicken. We're approaching the hangar now, and I need to get my bearings before we start another day of close quarters and charged moments.

But as I watch him greet the morning shift mechanics with that easy charm, I realize I'm fighting a losing battle against whatever this is becoming.

From around the corner of the hangar, I hear Ben's voice, engaged in what sounds like a tense phone call. I pause, not meaning to eavesdrop, but his words stop me cold.

"What do you mean another week? The storm system's that bad?" Ben's usual cheerful tone has an edge to it.

"No, I understand safety protocols, but... Yeah, I know. Nothing's flying in or out until it passes."

My stomach drops. *Another week?* The coffee and pancakes from earlier turn to lead in my gut.

"Alright, keep me posted if anything changes." Ben's footsteps approach, and I try to compose myself before he rounds the corner. His face falls when he sees me. "Ah, shit. You heard that?"

I nod, my mind already racing through calculations. "A week? That's..." My breath comes faster. "That's fifteen passengers. Hotel arrangements, missed connections, corporate's going to—"

"Hey, breathe." Ben steps closer. "These storms blow through pretty quick sometimes. The forecasts tend to overestimate—"

"Quick?" My laugh comes out sharp. "There's nothing quick about a week of delays. Do you know how many flights this impacts? The domino effect on schedules?" My hands shake as I pull out my phone. "I need to call dispatch, and the crew coordinator, and—"

"Nora." Ben's voice is firm but gentle. "Look at me."

I keep scrolling through my contacts, barely registering

his words. "The holiday season's coming up, we're already tight on personnel. This is going to be a nightmare to—"

Warm hands grip my shoulders, steadying me. I look up, startled by the contact, and find Ben's concerned gaze fixed on mine. Before I can process what's happening, he pulls me into his chest, wrapping his arms around me in a secure embrace.

My first instinct is to pull away – this is wildly inappropriate, he works for me, technically – but something in me crumbles instead. His warmth seeps through my uniform, and I find myself leaning into him, my forehead resting against his shoulder. He smells like coffee and motor oil and something woodsy I can't place.

"I've got you," he murmurs, one hand moving in slow circles on my back. "Just breathe with me for a minute."

I should step back. I should maintain professional boundaries. I should do a lot of things that don't involve standing in an airport hangar, being held by a mechanic whose muscled arms and intoxicating scent are making it impossible to think clearly. But his embrace feels like an anchor in the storm of my anxiety, and despite every professional instinct screaming at me to move away, my body betrays me by wanting to stay exactly where I am.

My breathing gradually syncs with his, and the steady rise and fall of his chest against mine sends a dangerous warmth through my body. The panic recedes, replaced by an electric awareness of every point of contact between us – his strong arms around my waist making my skin tingle beneath my uniform, my hands pressed against the firm planes of his back, the slight scratch of his work jacket against my cheek as I fight the urge to turn my face into his neck.

Time stretches, elastic and uncertain. Neither of us moves to break the embrace. If anything, his arms tighten fractionally, and I find myself melting further into him, my heart hammering against my ribs. The rational part of my brain knows we've been standing like this far too long, but my body has other ideas, craving more of this forbidden contact that's making me forget every reason why this is wrong.

A distant door slams somewhere in the hangar, the sound echoing off metal walls. Reality crashes back in, but still, we linger for one more breath, two, three, before slowly pulling apart. Ben's hands slide from my back to my arms, maintaining contact for a moment longer before dropping away.

His cheeks are flushed, and I'm sure mine match. We stand there, the space between us charged with something new and dangerous, neither quite able to meet the other's eyes.

I trail after Ben as he heads toward the plane, my feet moving of their own accord. My body still tingles from our embrace, and I can't seem to maintain a professional distance. Every few steps, my shoulder nearly brushes his arm.

"The replacement parts will be here, don't worry," Ben explains, but I'm barely processing his words. Instead, I'm noticing how his muscles flex as he gestures, the way his jaw works when he's thinking.

He pauses at the maintenance ladder, turning to face me. We're standing closer than strictly necessary, and his eyes widen slightly at our proximity. A slow smile spreads across his face.

"You know, for someone who was just panicking about delays, you seem pretty... distracted." His voice drops lower, taking on a teasing edge that sends heat rushing to my cheeks.

"I'm listening," I manage, but my voice sounds breathless even to my own ears.

"Really?" He leans against the ladder, crossing his arms.

The movement pulls his t-shirt tight across his chest. "So what did I just say about the fuel line?"

"I... um..."

"That's what I thought." He chuckles, and the sound does dangerous things to my insides. "Though I have to admit, I'm enjoying having your full attention – even if it's not on the technical details."

My mouth goes dry. *Is he actually flirting with me? Here? Now? After that embrace that I still can't stop thinking about?*

"The view's pretty good from where I'm standing too," he adds softly, his eyes traveling slowly down my uniform before meeting mine again.

The intensity of his gaze sets off alarm bells in my head. This is exactly what I was afraid of. One moment of weakness, letting him hold me, and now all my carefully maintained boundaries are crumbling.

"I should go check on the passengers," I blurt out, taking several quick steps backward. "Make sure everyone's settled with the new delay information."

"Nora, wait—"

But I'm already speed-walking across the hangar, my heart pounding. I don't stop until I reach the terminal building, putting several thick walls and a good hundred yards between us. Leaning against the cool concrete, I take deep breaths, trying to slow my racing pulse.

What am I doing? I'm a professional, a captain with fifteen years of experience. I can't be acting like some lovesick teenager just because a handsome mechanic gave me a hug and made eyes at me. No matter how good his arms felt around me, or how that smile makes my stomach flip, or how much I want to...

No. Stop. This ends now.

From now on, I'll maintain proper distance. Send other crew members to check on repair progress. Keep all communication strictly professional and preferably through email or phone.

I straighten my uniform and smooth my hair, rebuilding my captain's composure piece by piece. I have responsibilities, a reputation to maintain. I can't let whatever this is compromise everything I've worked for.

But as I head toward the ticket counter, I can still feel the phantom warmth of his embrace, still hear that low chuckle that made my knees weak. Running away might put physical distance between us, but my thoughts remain traitorously fixed on the man I left standing by that maintenance ladder.

CHAPTER FIVE

the snowstorm

NORA KRAMER

I STAND in front of my crew, maintaining my composure as I break the news about our situation. "The incoming storm has grounded us for two weeks. I need you to inform our passengers that we'll be providing accommodations in town until conditions improve."

Sarah, my head flight attendant, nods professionally but I catch the flash of concern in her eyes. "And the mechanical issues, Captain?"

"Ben—Mr. Huffman—says the repairs are nearly complete, but with this weather moving in..." I glance out the window at the threatening sky. "Safety first."

"I'll be staying at the Bed & Breakfast here by the hanger with some of the passengers, while you and the others check in at the hotel," I instruct her, adjusting my captain's jacket. The old Victorian building across the street has been a saving grace during previous weather delays - its owner always keeps a few rooms reserved for stranded flight crews. "Make sure everyone has the emergency contact numbers, and have them meet in the hotel lobby at eight tomorrow morning for updates. We'll coordinate transportation from there if needed."

After dismissing the crew, I head into town, the wind already picking up. The local outfitter's bell chimes as I push open the door, bringing with it the scent of leather and wool. The elderly shopkeeper looks up from his crossword puzzle.

"Storm's coming," he says, as if I haven't noticed the darkening sky. "Gonna be a bad one."

I select a down-filled jacket and a pair of snowshoes, remembering too many stories of stranded travelers. The shopkeeper rings up my purchases with methodical precision.

"Smart choice," he comments. "Better to have 'em and not need 'em."

Back in my hotel room, I hang the new jacket in the closet and prop the snowshoes by the door. The first flakes begin to fall as I gaze out my third-floor window. The hangar where Ben's been working on my plane is already locked down, metal doors sealed against the approaching storm. Lights are going out across town as businesses close early.

I lean my forehead against the cool window pane, watching the snowflakes grow thicker with each passing minute. This can't be happening. Not again. I should be landing in Anchorage right now, checking into the Hilton, maybe ordering room service and that glass of cabernet I've been craving since takeoff.

My phone buzzes - another weather alert. I don't need to look at it. The way the snow is coming down sideways tells me everything I need to know. My reflection in the window glass shows the tight line of my mouth, the furrow between my brows that I can't seem to smooth away.

"Perfect. Just perfect." I push away from the window and pace the small hotel room. The walls feel like they're closing in already. Last time I got grounded by weather like this, it was in Whitehorse. Fourteen days of watching the snow pile up outside my window, each day bringing another cancellation notice. Fourteen days of my carefully structured life completely derailed.

The heating unit kicks on with a rattle that makes me jump. This place is a far cry from the Hilton. The bedspread has a pattern straight out of 1985, and the bathroom door sticks when you try to close it. At least the sheets smell clean.

I pull out my tablet, checking the weather radar for the thousandth time. The storm system spans hundreds of miles, a massive swirl of blue and purple that's parked itself right over us. My finger traces the edge of it, searching for any sign it might move on quickly, but the forecast is grim. High pressure to the north, low pressure to the south - this thing isn't going anywhere.

"Two weeks," I mutter, dropping onto the bed. "Please, not two weeks."

The sound of a snow plow rumbling past draws me back to the window. Through the thickening white, I can just make out the town's main street. The few pedestrians still out are hurrying along, heads down against the wind. A figure in a thick work coat catches my eye - Ben, leaving the hangar. Even from here, I can see how the wind buffets him as he makes his way to his truck.

My chest tightens watching him. He'd been so confident earlier about fixing the mechanical issues, his hands sure and capable as he worked. "Just a few more hours, Captain," he'd said, flashing that easy smile that makes him look even younger than his twenty-eight years. Now those repairs won't matter until this weather breaks.

I sink into the room's sole armchair and pull close to the heater. The wind howls outside, rattling the window in its frame. My phone lights up with a text from dispatch - all flights are grounded for at least the next 48 hours. I close my eyes, remembering the Whitehorse incident. Day after day of watching my schedule disintegrate, of calling to reschedule connecting flights, of trying to keep my crew's morale up while my own patience wore thinner and thinner.

The room feels suffocating suddenly. I grab my new jacket and room key, needing to move, to do something besides sit here and watch snow fall. The hallway is quiet - most of my passengers have probably holed up in their rooms already. Smart of them. But I've never been good at sitting still when things go wrong.

In the lobby, the desk clerk looks up from her computer. "Captain Kramer? You're not thinking of going out in this?"

"Just to the coffee shop across the street," I say, zipping

up the jacket. "I need something stronger than what's in the room."

She gives me a look that clearly questions my sanity. "The Moose Mug closed early. Everything's shutting down for the storm."

Of course it is. Because that's exactly how my luck is running today. I stand there for a moment, feeling the weight of being trapped pressing down on me. Whitehorse all over again. Except this time I'm in an even smaller town, with even fewer options for distraction.

The desk clerk must see something in my expression because her voice softens. "We've got some decent coffee in the breakfast room. It's not fancy, but it's hot."

I nod my thanks and change course. The breakfast room is deserted, chairs turned up on tables for the night. The coffee machine hums in the corner, and the smell of burnt coffee fills the air. I pour a cup, not expecting much, and settle into a chair by the window.

From here, I can see the airport's beacon flashing through the snow, a steady rhythm that usually means home to me. Now it just reminds me of how stuck I am. The coffee tastes exactly as bad as it smells, but I drink it anyway, watching the snow erase the world outside.

My mind drifts back to my last conversation with Ben. He'd seemed genuinely disappointed when he heard about the incoming storm, like he'd been looking forward to spending more time working on the plane. *Or maybe, a small voice whispers, looking forward to spending more time around you.* I push that thought away immediately. He's just being professional, and besides, he's far too young to...

The lights flicker, making me tense. Not just stuck, but possibly stuck in the dark if this keeps up. I should have packed my emergency kit in my carry-on instead of checking it through to Anchorage. Rookie mistake. Fifteen years of flying, and somehow the universe still finds ways to humble me.

My phone buzzes again - Sarah, checking in about the passengers. I tap out a quick response, grateful for the distraction. Keep everyone calm, make sure they're comfortable, standard protocol. We've been through this before, if not quite in such a remote location.

The wind picks up another notch, howling around the building's corners like a living thing. The snow is so thick now I can barely see the streetlights. The coffee cup is empty, but I keep holding it, letting the last traces of warmth seep into my fingers.

Two weeks in Whitehorse nearly drove me crazy. *How long will we be stuck here?* The thought of spending days in this tiny hotel room makes my skin crawl. I'm used to movement, to action, to being in control of my destination. Being grounded like this feels like having my wings clipped.

I stand up, tossing the empty cup in the trash. Might as well try to get some sleep, even though my body clock is completely confused about what time zone it's in. As I head back toward the elevator, I hear the wind rattle the front doors hard enough to make the desk clerk look up nervously.

"Going to be a long night," she says sympathetically.

I manage a tight smile. "Going to be a long several nights, from the looks of it."

The elevator creaks its way up to my floor, and I try not to think about being trapped in here if the power goes out. Back in my room, I change into yoga pants and a soft sweater, grateful I always pack extra clothes in my pilot's bag. The gas fireplace flickers to life with a push of a button, and I'm just about to settle into the armchair with my tablet when there's a knock at the door.

My heart skips when I look through the peephole and see Ben standing there, snowflakes melting in his dark hair. I shouldn't open the door. I'm his client, he's my mechanic, and there are a dozen other reasons why this is a bad idea.

I open it anyway.

"Hey," he says, looking surprisingly uncertain for someone usually so confident. "I wanted to check on you, make sure you're set for the storm."

"Come in," I say, stepping aside. "It's getting nasty out there."

Ben runs a hand through his damp hair as he enters, and I catch the fresh scent of snow and pine. He's changed out of his work clothes into jeans and a flannel shirt that makes him look even younger than his twenty-eight years.

"Can I get you some tea?" I offer, mostly to have something to do with my hands. I thought about the awful coffee I had downstairs and was glad to have something here to offer. "The hotel left some in the room."

"Sure, thanks." He settles onto the couch while I busy myself with the electric kettle. "The hangar's all secured, by the way. Your plane will be fine."

"I saw from the window." I hand him a steaming cup and sit in the armchair, maintaining a safe distance. "Thank you for checking in."

We sip our tea in comfortable silence for a moment, watching the snow through the window. The wind howls outside, making the warmth of the room feel more intimate.

"You know," Ben starts, then pauses. "I didn't just come here to check on you because of the storm."

My hands tighten around my mug. "Oh?"

"I've been thinking about my life lately," he continues, looking into his tea. "Everyone expects me to follow this certain path because I'm young, like I should be out partying or jumping from job to job. But I love what I do. I know exactly what I want."

"There's nothing wrong with that," I say softly.

"What about you?" He looks up, his gaze direct. "Do you ever feel like people have expectations that don't match who you really are?"

The question hits closer to home than I'd like to admit. "Sometimes. People see the uniform, the captain's stripes, and they think they know everything about me. They don't see…"

"The woman who takes a chance on a young mechanic?" His eyes drift appreciatively over my figure. "Who's smart enough to buy snowshoes just in case? Who looks absolutely stunning in that captain's uniform, and whose eyes sparkle when she talks about flying?"

I feel the heat rise to my cheeks, both from his words and the way he's looking at me. "Ben..."

"I can't stop thinking about you, Nora." He sets his cup down and leans forward, close enough that I catch the spicy scent of his aftershave. "I know there are fifteen years between us. I know you probably think I'm too young or that this is crazy." His voice drops lower, sending a shiver down my spine. "But when I'm with you, age doesn't matter. All that matters is how my heart races when you're near me, how I can barely focus on repairs when you're watching me work, how badly I want to know if your lips are as soft as they look."

My heart pounds as he moves to sit beside me on the arm of my chair. "This is complicated," I whisper.

"Life is complicated," he says. "But this? This feels simple."

When he leans down, I don't pull away. His lips meet mine tentatively at first, a question more than a demand. I answer by reaching up to cup his face, drawing him closer. The kiss deepens, and I feel years of carefully maintained control beginning to crack.

We break apart, both breathing heavily. Ben rests his forehead against mine, and I close my eyes, trying to process the surge of emotions coursing through me.

CHAPTER SIX

stay the night

NORA KRAMER

I STARE into the glittering pattern of the flames in the fireplace as Ben's lips leave mine, my heart racing from our first tentative kiss that rapidly transformed into something far more intense. The warmth from the fire can't compete with the heat building between us.

Through the window, the snow is falling harder now, creating a cocoon of white that seems to separate us from the rest of the world. The soft patter against the glass creates a hypnotic rhythm that matches my quickening pulse.

"You're incredible," Ben whispers, his fingers tracing along my jawline. His touch is reverent, gentle yet confident. My body responds to him in ways I haven't experienced in years, maybe ever.

"This has to stay between us," I say softly, meeting his gaze. The responsibility of my position weighs heavily, even as my resolve weakens. "Just us."

Ben nods, his eyes serious. "I understand. I would never do anything to compromise your career or reputation."

Taking his hand, I lead him toward the bedroom. The room is bathed in the ethereal glow from the storm outside, snowflakes dancing past the window like stardust. We lie down together on the plush comforter, shoulders touching as we watch nature's display outside.

"It's beautiful," I whisper, though I'm hardly looking at the snow anymore. Ben turns to face me, and I see my own wonder reflected in his eyes. His fingers intertwine with mine, and the simple touch sends electricity through my entire body.

When our lips meet again, it's different from before — slower, deeper, his tongue dancing with mine. My hands find their way to his chest as his arms wrap around me, pulling me closer. The world outside fades away until there's nothing left but this moment, this connection that defies all my careful rules and expectations.

The snowstorm rages on outside, but in here, we create our own kind of weather. Every touch, every kiss builds like gathering storm clouds, leading us toward an inevitable crescendo.

I moan softly into Ben's mouth as his hands roam over my body, his fingers tracing delicate paths along my spine and over my hips. I can feel the heat between us growing more intense with every passing moment, the air thick with anticipation.

Our lips part reluctantly as we both catch our breath, but the connection between us is tangible even as we pull away. I look into Ben's eyes, seeing a mix of desire and vulnerability that takes my breath away.

Without a word, Ben begins to undress, his movements fluid and confident as he peels off his shirt and pants, revealing the muscular form that I've been admiring all night. I can't help but feel a shiver of desire as I take in the sight of him, the firelight casting long shadows across his skin.

Without hesitation, I follow his lead, stripping off my own clothes and revealing my own body to him. I watch as his eyes roam over me, drinking in the sight of my curves and the lines of my body. His fingers trace over my skin, exploring every inch as he whispers words of admiration and desire.

As we move closer together, our bodies coming into contact once more, the passion between us ignites with a fiery intensity. I can feel Ben's hardness pressing against me, a reminder of just how much we both want each other.

His lips find mine once more, kissing me hungrily as his hands roam over my body, exploring every inch with a sense of urgency. I respond in kind, my own hands grasping at him, pulling him closer as I lose myself in the sensation of his touch.

Before long, our clothes are discarded in a heap on the floor, leaving us both completely naked. As we lie down together, the warmth of our bodies melding together, I can feel the anticipation building between us like a coiled spring.

Ben's lips trace a path down my neck, his tongue teasing the sensitive skin as he nips gently at my collarbone. I moan softly, my hips arching towards him as his touch sends waves of pleasure through my body.

As his mouth moves lower, exploring the delicate lines of my chest, I feel a sense of vulnerability that is both terrifying and exhilarating. But Ben's touch is gentle, loving, and I can't help but relax into his embrace as he suckles at my breasts, his tongue flicking over my nipples.

My fingers entwine in his hair, guiding him as he continues to explore my body, his mouth moving lower still. I feel a shiver of anticipation as his lips reach my abdomen, kissing and sucking gently at my skin as he makes his way lower.

I stop him ... I like to be in control and roll him around until I'm positioned above him, my legs straddling his hips. His eyes lock with mine, filled with anticipation as I reach down and grip his erection. With a firm yet gentle touch, I stroke him slowly, enjoying the feel of his hard length in my hands. Ben lets out a low moan, clearly enjoying the sensation.

I can't believe I'm doing this. I've never been one to abandon protocol, but the passion building between us is too intense to resist. I lower myself down, my eyes locked on Ben's, and feel the heat of his arousal against my bare folds.

As I lower myself further, taking him into me, Ben's breath hitches and his grip on my waist tightens. His eyes roll back in pleasure as he lets out a guttural moan. His hands move to my ass, squeezing and pulling me closer, driving him deeper into me.

I brace myself against the mattress, feeling every inch of him stretching me as he fills me completely. He groans, the sound vibrating through my body, intensifying the sensation.

Our rhythm becomes frenzied; Ben's hips undulate beneath me, pushing into me with long, hard strokes that make my head spin. His teeth graze at my neck, sending shivers down my spine and fuelling the fire raging inside me.

I lean forward, my breasts brushing against his chest as my hips move in perfect sync with his. Our moans and grunts fill the room, the only sound besides the storm outside. He grabs at both at my breasts, licking one and the the other.

The taste of his skin, the smell of his hair, envelope me as I lose myself in the moment. My nails dig into his shoulders, pulling him closer, urging him on. His fingers find my clit, teasing and circling as he thrusts deeper.

The tension builds, winding tighter and tighter until it feels like it might snap. I cry out as the first wave of pleasure washes over me, my body arching into his touch.

Ben follows closely behind, his muscles tensing beneath me as he grunts out a primal growl. He holds me tighter still, his thrusts harder and deeper, his fingers finding their way inside me as he chases yet another orgasm.

We collapse together, tangled in a heap of sweat-slick limbs, our breathing ragged from the intensity of the encounter. Ben's chest heaves against mine, his lips finding my ear. "I've never wanted anyone like I want you," he murmurs, his voice rough with emotion.

I can't help but feel the same, despite the age gap and our professions. This moment with Ben feels like a glimpse into a different universe, one where passion and desire rule above all else. I trace his jawline with my fingers, feeling the stubble beneath my fingertips.

We lie together for a while, catching our breath and basking in the afterglow. The storm outside rages on, but it feels like we're the only two people in the world. Finally, I lean in and press a soft kiss to Ben's lips, tasting myself on him. "That was ..."

"Incredible," he finishes for me, his voice full of awe.

Ben's arms envelop me, his warmth seeping into my body as he plants a gentle kiss on my forehead. I let out a contented sigh, the rhythm of his heart beating against my cheek. My fingers trace along the muscles of his back, reveling in the feeling of his skin beneath my touch.

After a moment of comfortable silence, I glance out the window, my eyes drawn to the relentless snowfall outside.

When I speak, my voice is thick with a mix of exhaustion and pleasure. "Your truck must be covered by now."

Ben follows my gaze, a small smile playing at the corners of his mouth. "You might be right."

I hesitate for a moment before letting the words slip from my lips. "It's probably best if you stay the night."

The relief in Ben's expression is visible, his smile growing wider as he nods in agreement. Inside, I can't help but feel a thrill of anticipation at the thought of having him close to me for the rest of the evening.

"I haven't been with anyone for five years," I confess, closing my eyes against the vulnerability of the admission. The words feel strange leaving my lips - it's not something I've said out loud before, not even to myself. My heart pounds a little faster, knowing I've just shared something so intimate with Ben, but there's also a peculiar sense of relief in finally acknowledging it.

As we lie together, the weight of my confession hangs in the air between us. I hadn't planned on telling him about my celibacy, but something about Ben's presence makes me feel safe – like I can share this part of myself without fear of judgment. Despite the intimacy we've just shared, I can't shake the feeling that there is still so much more I want to know about him.

My hand wanders down the length of his torso, coming to rest on the firm muscles of his thigh. I can't help but notice the way his breath hitches as my fingers trace along the contours of his body. Embracing my boldness, I let my hand wander further, gently grasping his penis as it begins to stir to life once more.

To my surprise, Ben lets out a soft chuckle. "I would've never guessed," he says, his voice thick with desire. He doesn't question my confession, doesn't push for an explanation. Instead, we find ourselves carried away by the silent understanding that passes between us.

As we make love for the second time that night, the storm outside continues to rage, its fury mirrored by the passion that builds between us. Our movements become more urgent, our breaths mingled and ragged as we cling to one another, desperate for the release that only comes from the intimate connection we've found.

The steady rhythm of Ben's hips rocks my world, each thrust pushing me closer to the precipice of ecstasy. I can feel my body surrendering to the pleasure, my muscles tensing as I dig my nails into the strong muscles of his back.

As the first waves of my orgasm crash over me, I cry out his name, the sound of it still foreign on my lips. Yet there is something undeniable about the way that it rolls off my tongue, like the sweetest of secrets whispered into the darkness.

Ben follows me over the edge, his own release coming moments later with a guttural groan. We cling to one another, our bodies entwined as we ride out the last vestiges of our shared pleasure.

When it's over, we lay together, our limbs tangled and our breathing gradually slowing. It's as if the storm outside has passed, leaving in its wake a serene calm that settles over us like a comforting embrace.

As I drift off to sleep, my head resting on Ben's chest, I realize that this is the first time in years I've felt truly at peace. The weight of my responsibilities – the expectations and the pressure – all of it seemed to fade away into the background, drowned out by the steady beat of his heart. And as I surrender to the sweet embrace of slumber, I can't help but wonder what the morning will bring.

CHAPTER SEVEN
missed calls
NORA KRAMER

I WAKE SLOWLY, cocooned in warmth despite the chill in the air. My eyes flutter open to find Ben's arm draped across my waist, his steady breathing tickling the back of my neck. The room is dim, almost dark, and when I squint toward the windows, all I see is white. Snow has completely covered them, blocking out any natural light.

I lie perfectly still, savoring the weight of Ben's arm across my body and the gentle rhythm of his breathing. What surprises me most isn't the fact that I spent the night with a younger man - it's how completely at peace I feel about it. No panic, no regret, just a deep sense of contentment that seems to radiate from my core.

The room is eerily quiet, muffled by what must be feet of accumulated snow outside. Through the darkness, I can make out the faint outline of snowflakes still falling beyond the window, their shapes barely visible in the grey pre-dawn light. The storm hasn't let up. We're probably snowed in, but for once in my life, being grounded doesn't fill me with that familiar anxiety.

This should feel wrong, I think to myself, but it doesn't. Not even close.

Ben shifts slightly in his sleep, pulling me closer. His skin is warm against mine, and I can't resist running my fingers lightly along his arm, tracing the defined muscles. For someone who works with heavy machinery all day, his touch last night had been surprisingly gentle, almost reverent.

I allow my hand to explore further, skimming down his side to rest on his hip. Even in sleep, he's gorgeous - all lean muscle and smooth skin. His dark hair is tousled, falling across his forehead in a way that makes him look younger than his twenty-eight years. But age seems like such an arbitrary thing now, here in this cocoon of warmth we've created.

My pilot's brain, always calculating, tries to assess the situation logically. Fifteen years between us. Professional boundaries crossed. Potential complications when we return to our regular lives. But for every potential problem, there's a counterargument that feels just as valid. His maturity. The genuine connection we share. The way he sees me - not as some authority figure to be impressed, but as a woman he actually wants to know.

A particularly strong gust of wind rattles the window, making the snow tap against the glass like tiny fingers. The sound should remind me of all my responsibilities waiting outside, but instead, it only reinforces how protected I feel in this moment. I can't remember the last time I felt this... *safe*. This understood.

Ben's breathing changes slightly, and his hand twitches against my waist. I freeze, not wanting to wake him yet. There's something precious about this private moment of observation, this chance to simply exist in the same space without any need for words or explanations.

I study his face in the dim light - the strong line of his jaw, the slight curve of his lips, the faint shadow of stubble along his cheeks. Last night, those lips had traced paths across my skin that made me forget everything except the sensation of his touch. Now, relaxed in sleep, he looks peaceful, almost vulnerable.

My fingers continue their exploration, trailing along his collarbone, down his chest. His skin is smooth and warm under my touch. I'm mapping him, memorizing every plane and curve, as if some part of me needs to prove this is real and not just some vivid dream born of isolation and attraction.

The professional part of my brain tries one last time to raise objections, but they feel hollow now. I've spent so many years building walls, maintaining control, keeping everyone at a safe distance. But Ben had somehow slipped past all my defenses with nothing more than honest conversation and genuine interest in who I am beneath the captain's uniform.

A small smile plays at the corners of my mouth as I remember how adamantly I'd resisted his initial attempts to show me around town. How certain I'd been that he was too young, too casual, too different from my carefully ordered world. Now, just days later, I'm lying here wondering how I ever thought age could matter more than this profound sense of connection.

The wind howls outside, and I burrow closer to Ben's warmth. The storm has probably shut down the entire town, but for the first time in my career, being grounded feels like a gift rather than a punishment. Time has become something precious rather than something to race against.

His arm tightens around me unconsciously, and I let my head rest against his chest, listening to the steady thump of his heartbeat. There's something almost magical about this moment - the silence, the darkness, the sense of being completely cut off from the world outside. It's as if we've found our own private universe where the usual rules don't apply.

I trace lazy patterns on his skin, marveling at how natural this feels. There's none of the awkwardness I'd expected, none of the morning-after regret I'd braced myself for. Instead, there's just this profound sense of rightness, of pieces falling into place that I hadn't even known were missing.

The storm continues its assault outside, but in here, we're suspended in a moment of perfect calm. I know eventually we'll have to face reality - my crew, his colleagues, the complicated logistics of whatever this is becoming. But right now, in this quiet space between night and morning, I allow myself to simply exist in this moment, treasuring the feeling of being completely, utterly at peace.

Ben stirs slightly, and I hold my breath, still not ready to break this spell. His breathing remains steady, and I release the air from my lungs slowly, carefully. I want to preserve this moment just a little longer, to stay in this space where everything feels possible and nothing needs to be defined or explained.

For a moment, I allow myself to sink into this peaceful feeling, to savor the solid presence of his body against mine. But then my pilot's instincts kick in - something's not right about the light, or lack thereof. I reach for my phone on the nightstand and my heart nearly stops.

"Oh god," I bolt upright, startling Ben awake. "Ten missed calls from Sarah."

Ben stirs beside me, running a hand through his tousled hair. "What time is it?"

"Two in the afternoon." I scroll through the notifications, my stomach dropping. "Sarah's been trying to reach me all morning about the storm conditions."

"Afternoon?" Ben grabs his own phone and curses. "Shit. Liam's called three times too. I never sleep through calls."

I pull the sheet around me, suddenly very aware of my state of undress and the reality of what happened last night. Ben's hand finds my lower back, his touch sending warmth through my skin.

"Hey," he says softly. "Don't spiral. The storm's got everything shut down anyway."

I turn to look at him, and my breath catches. In the dim light, his features are softer, but his eyes hold the same intensity they did last night. The same care and desire that made me throw caution to the wind.

"I should call Sarah back," I say, but I don't move.

Ben sits up, the sheet pooling around his waist. "We should probably talk about... this. Us."

"Us." The word feels foreign on my tongue. "Ben, last night was..."

"Amazing," he finishes, and the certainty in his voice makes my heart skip. "And not just the physical part. Talking with you, being with you - I've never connected with someone like this."

I find myself nodding. "I know what you mean. It's like..." I search for the words. "Like we speak the same language. Despite..."

"The age difference?" He raises an eyebrow. "Nora, I meant what I said last night. I don't care about that."

"But others will," I say, voicing the fear that's been gnawing at me. "The airline has strict fraternization policies. And even if they didn't, people *will* talk. They'll assume things about both of us."

"Let them talk." Ben shifts closer, taking my hand. "I'm not ashamed of how I feel about you. I'm not some kid with a crush. What I feel is real."

"My crew already suspects something," I admit. "Sarah gave me this look yesterday when I mentioned your name."

"Liam figured it out too." Ben chuckles. "He's been texting me about the 'hot pilot' since day one."

Despite my anxiety, I laugh. "Really?"

"Really. He thinks I should go for it. Says I've been smiling like an idiot every time I talk about you."

I squeeze his hand. "We both have careers to think about. Reputations."

"And we'll figure that out," he says with that quiet confidence that drew me to him in the first place. "But right now, we're snowed in, the world is white, and I'm exactly where I want to be."

"With a woman fifteen years your senior?" I can't help but ask.

"With a brilliant pilot who challenges me, makes me laugh, and happens to be gorgeous." He traces my jawline with his free hand. "Age is just a number, Nora. What matters is how we feel when we're together."

The conviction in his voice melts my defenses. "And how do you feel?"

"Like I've found something rare. Something worth fighting for." His eyes hold mine. "I know we've only known each other a few days, but sometimes you just know. You know?"

I do know. It's terrifying and exhilarating all at once. "The aviation community is small," I warn. "Word travels fast."

"Then let it travel. I'm not interested in hiding how I feel about you. Unless..." He hesitates for the first time. "Unless that's what you want?"

"No," I say, surprising myself with how quickly and firmly the word comes out. "No, I don't want to hide. I'm just... scared. Of what this could mean. For both of us."

"We take it one day at a time," he says, pulling me closer. "Right now, we're grounded by a snowstorm. We have time to figure things out."

I reluctantly pull away from Ben's warmth, wrapping the sheet around me as I grab my phone. Sarah answers on the first ring.

"Finally! Where have you been? I've been worried sick!"

"Sorry, Sarah. The storm knocked out my alarm." The lie comes easily, though guilt pricks at my conscience. "I just woke up."

"Well, we're completely snowed in. The airport's closed, and they're saying we might be stuck here for another week or two." Her voice carries a mix of concern and curiosity. "Are you okay? You sound... different."

"I'm fine. Just catching up on some much-needed rest." I watch Ben grab his own phone and step into the bathroom, his muscled back disappearing behind the door. "Keep me posted on any updates from dispatch?"

"Of course. But Nora..." Sarah pauses. "You'd tell me if something was going on, right?"

"Nothing to tell," I say, knowing my voice betrays me. "Stay warm, Sarah."

I end the call just as Ben's voice drifts from the bathroom. "No, Liam, I'm fine. The shop's closed anyway... Yes, I know about the Anderson job... It can wait until the roads are clear."

There's a pause, and I can hear the muffled sound of his brother's voice through the phone.

"That's none of your business," Ben says, but I can hear the smile in his voice. "I'll call you later... Yes, I'm being careful... Goodbye, Liam."

He emerges from the bathroom, and our eyes meet. A grin spreads across his face, matching my own. Something about the absurdity of the situation - two grown adults hiding from phone calls like teenagers - breaks through my usual reserve.

"Did Sarah buy your story?" Ben asks, crossing the room with deliberate slowness.

"About as much as Liam bought yours." I can't help the giggle that escapes - when was the last time I actually giggled?

"So, not at all?" He reaches the bed, his fingers finding the edge of the sheet I'm clutching.

"Not even a little bit." I release my grip on the fabric, letting it fall as Ben pulls me into his arms.

"Good thing we're snowed in then." His lips find my neck, and I shiver despite the warmth of his touch. "No one can expect us to go anywhere."

"Mmm, very convenient," I murmur, running my hands over his chest. "Almost like the weather's conspiring to keep us here."

"I should send Mother Nature a thank you note." Ben guides us back toward the bed, his movements unhurried but purposeful.

We fall onto the mattress together, laughing as we get tangled in the sheets. There's none of the hesitation from last night, none of the careful testing of boundaries. Instead, there's just joy and desire and the pure pleasure of being together.

Ben pulls the covers over us, creating our own private world away from the storm and responsibilities and all the complications waiting outside. His body aligns perfectly with mine, and I marvel again at how natural this feels, how right.

"So," he whispers against my skin, "about that much-needed rest..."

I thread my fingers through his hair, pulling him closer. "I think we've rested enough, don't you?"

CHAPTER EIGHT
we need food
BEN HUFFMAN

I LIE IN BED, watching the snowflakes dance outside the window, their shadows casting delicate patterns across Nora's sleeping form. The storm rages on, but in here, everything is quiet, peaceful. My fingers trace invisible lines in the air above her bare shoulder, not quite touching, afraid to wake her.

How did I get here? Just days ago, I was fixing a Cessna's landing gear, another ordinary Thursday at the hangar. Then Jerry called about a pilot needing emergency maintenance, and there she was – Captain Nora Kramer, all sharp edges and professional poise, looking at me like I was some kid who'd wandered into her cockpit.

Now she's curled against my chest, her breathing deep

and even, dark hair spilling across my pillow. I still can't believe this is real.

"You're just a mechanic," I whisper to myself, testing how the words feel. But that's not what Nora saw. She saw past the grease-stained coveralls and my age, saw something in me worth taking a chance on.

My mind drifts to Jodi, my first real girlfriend from tech school. We dated for two years, but it was always comfortable, predictable. Then Paulina, the flight attendant who breezed through town last summer. That burned hot and fast, all passion and no substance.

This thing with Nora? It's different. When she talks about flying, her eyes light up with the same fire I feel when I'm elbow-deep in an engine, solving a problem everyone else gave up on. She gets it. Gets me.

A particularly strong gust rattles the window, and Nora stirs slightly. I hold my breath, but she just burrows deeper into the blankets. My heart clenches at the sight.

What is this feeling? It's like someone's rewired my entire system. Every time she laughs at one of my dumb jokes or challenges my repair assessment with her pilot's knowledge, something clicks into place. When she kissed me earlier, it felt like coming home to a place I didn't even know I was missing.

The snow's really coming down now, thick white curtains obscuring the world outside. Part of me hopes it never stops, that we stay trapped in this moment where age is just a number and job titles don't matter. But the rational part of my brain knows better. She has a career, responsibilities. A life that doesn't include small-town Alaska mechanics.

I think about how she looked at sunset yesterday, wind whipping her hair around her face as she took in the view from Miller's Point. She belonged there, wild and free, just like she belongs in the sky. And now she's here, in my arms, and I'm terrified of pressing too hard, of wanting too much.

Jodi used to say I lived too much in my head, always analyzing, always trying to understand the mechanics of everything. But this isn't something I can diagnose with a wrench and a manual. This feeling – God, I might as well call it what it is – *this love*, it's beyond anything I've experienced.

The word catches in my throat. **Love.** Is that what this is? It seems impossible – we've known each other for days, not weeks or months or years. **Days.** But when I look at her, everything else fades away. The age gap, the different worlds we come from, none of it matters.

The buzz of my phone interrupts my thoughts. Liam. Again. I let it go to voicemail, not ready to deal with his reaction. My little brother's always been my biggest cheerleader when it comes to relationships, but this is different. This isn't some local girl from the bar or a tourist passing through.

I can already hear his voice: "Bro, you're dating a pilot? An older woman? That's legendary!" He'd probably high-five me, make some inappropriate joke about cockpits, then ask for all the details. That's Liam – zero filter, all enthusiasm.

Nora shifts beside me, and I hold still, watching her face for signs of waking. She doesn't. The corner of her mouth twitches in sleep, and I wonder what she's dreaming about.

Growing up, Liam always said I had some kind of magic with women. "It's not fair," he'd complain after watching another girl slip me her number at the diner. "You don't even try." He never understood that was exactly why – I never played games, never put on an act. I was just... me.

But those other connections? They were surface-level, fleeting. Like the time Jenny from the hardware store asked me out. We dated for three months, and I can barely remember what we talked about. Or Kate, the ski instructor who spent a season here. She was fun, uncomplicated. We both knew it had an expiration date.

My phone buzzes again. This time it's a text.

> Dude, where are you? Town's completely snowed in. You better not be stuck at the hangar.

I type back quickly:

> I'm safe. Don't worry.

Three dots appear immediately:

> You're with her, aren't you? The pilot?

Classic Liam. Nothing gets past him. I set the phone face-down without responding, but I can imagine him pacing his apartment, bursting with questions. He's probably already crafted some dramatic romance novel version of events in his head.

The thing is, he wouldn't be entirely wrong. This does feel like something out of a story – the stranded pilot, the small-town mechanic, a snowstorm forcing them together. But it's real. So real it scares me.

Another text:

> You want me to save you?

I cringe at his words. Trust Liam to reduce something profound to locker room talk. But then again, maybe I'm being unfair. He's always supported my choices, even when they made no sense to anyone else. Like when I turned down that job offer in Seattle to stay here and take over Jerry's shop. Everyone thought I was crazy, but Liam? He got it.

"You've got to follow your gut," he told me then. "When something feels right, you know it."

And this – lying here with Nora, listening to her breathe, feeling like my heart might explode – this feels more right than anything ever has.

My phone lights up again:

> At least tell me if she's as hot naked as in that pilot's uniform.

I almost laugh out loud. There's the Liam I know, trying to drag this back into familiar territory. But how do I explain that Nora's beauty has nothing to do with uniforms or conventional attractiveness? It's in the way she commands a room without saying a word. The sharp intelligence in her eyes when she's processing new information. The rare, genuine smile that transforms her whole face.

Another message pops up:

> Mom's gonna flip when she finds out.

That stops my mental wandering cold. **Mom.** I hadn't even thought about her reaction. She's always wanted me to "settle down with a nice girl," but I doubt this is what she had in mind. She'll focus on the age gap, worry about what people will say. Small towns run on gossip, and Mom's never been good at ignoring it.

But then I look at Nora again, and something settles in my chest. Let them talk. Let them whisper and speculate and judge. None of it matters.

The snow keeps falling outside, thick and silent. In here, Nora sleeps on, unaware of my inner dialogue or Liam's rapid-fire texts. I reach for my phone one last time.

> Text later

She shifts again, and this time her eyes flutter open slightly. For a moment, she looks confused, then her face softens into a smile that makes my chest ache.

"Ben?" she murmurs, voice thick with sleep.

"I'm here," I whisper back, finally letting my fingers brush against her shoulder. Her skin is warm, real.

"What time is it?"

I glance at the bedside clock. "Just past midnight."

She hums contentedly and closes her eyes again. Before she drifts off, her hand finds mine under the covers, fingers intertwining naturally, like they've done this a thousand times before.

And that's when I know for sure – I don't want her to leave. Not tomorrow, not next week, not ever. The thought of her flying away, back to her regular routes and her normal life, feels like someone's ripping something essential from my chest.

I MUST HAVE DOZED off at some point because the next thing I know, warm sunlight is streaming through the window, painting golden stripes across the bed. Nora stirs beside me at the same moment, her eyes opening to meet mine.

"The storm," she says, sitting up. "It's stopped."

I follow her gaze to the window where blue sky peeks through scattered clouds. After the howling winds of last night, the silence feels almost unnatural. Nora's already sliding out of bed, her movements quick and purposeful as she gathers her clothes.

"I'm absolutely starving," she admits, pulling on her sweater. "When was the last time we ate?"

"Yesterday afternoon, I think." I grab my jeans from where they landed on the armchair. "Hotel serves breakfast until noon. Best pancakes in town, if you're interested."

She shoots me a playful look. "Lead the way, Mr. Huffman."

Something feels off the moment we step into the hallway. The usual morning bustle of housekeeping carts and guest chatter is absent. Our footsteps echo against the hardwood floors, the sound bouncing off empty walls.

"Where is everyone?" Nora's voice drops to a whisper.

I shake my head, picking up my pace toward the stairs. The third-floor landing is deserted, and so is the second. By the time we reach the lobby, my heart's racing, though I'm not sure why. The front desk stands empty, the morning newspaper undelivered.

"Maybe they're all in the dining room?" But even as I say it, I know something's wrong. The usual breakfast smells – coffee, bacon, fresh bread – are notably absent.

"What time is it?" Nora asks, pulling out her cell phone from her pocket. "Gee, it's only nine—where is everyone?"

I take the lead through the swinging doors into the kitchen, Nora close behind me. The industrial-sized space is cold and dark. No prep cooks chopping vegetables. No servers filling coffee urns. No line cooks working the griddle. Just silence and the lingering smell of yesterday's meals.

"Ben." Nora's voice has that same steady tone she used when we first discovered the mechanical issue with her plane. "Look outside."

I cross to the windows, my boots squeaking against the tile floor. For a moment, my brain can't process what I'm seeing. Where there should be a view of Main Street, there's just... white. Pure, unbroken white, rising well above the windowsill.

"That's not possible," I breathe, pressing my hand against the cold glass. But it is possible. The snow has completely entombed us, piling six, maybe eight feet high against the building's walls.

"We're snowed in," Nora states flatly.

I turn to face her, taking in the kitchen's dark expanse. No staff. No food prep. No deliveries. Just us and God knows how many other guests, trapped in this boutique hotel until the plows can dig us out.

The realization hits me like a punch to the gut: this isn't just a heavy snowfall. This is the kind of storm they write about in history books. The kind that changes things. And we're stuck right in the middle of it.

I look at Nora, her face illuminated by the strange, filtered light coming through the snow-covered windows. "I guess pancakes are off the menu."

"No," I say to her, trying to inject some optimism into my voice despite our predicament, "We're gonna cook them. You know how to cook?" I move toward the industrial stainless steel range, running my hand along the cold surface. Even in this crisis, there's something exciting about the prospect of taking over a professional kitchen, though I'd never admit that out loud.

CHAPTER NINE
a small gathering
NORA KRAMER

I WATCH Ben move methodically around the kitchen and dining room, his strong hands testing each window latch with careful precision. There's something deeply attractive about the way he takes charge of our safety, especially as the storm intensifies outside. The wind howls against the glass, but his presence makes the room feel like a fortress.

"This one's a bit loose," he says, jiggling the frame of the window nearest the small table. His brow furrows in concentration as he examines the mechanism. "Nothing to worry about, but we should probably put something in front of it just in case."

I pull myself up from a chair, wrapping my sweater

tighter around my shoulders. "How about another chair?"

Ben's already moving the chair to block the window. His movements are efficient, purposeful. It's the same focus I noticed when he was working on my plane, but now it's directed at protecting us from the elements. My chest tightens with an unfamiliar warmth.

"The door frame's solid," he continues, running his hand along the weather stripping. "But we should keep some extra towels ready in case any snow blows under."

I grab the spare towels from a nearby storeroom, our fingers brushing as I hand them to him. Even that small contact sends electricity through my skin. "You've done this before," I observe.

He flashes that easy smile that first caught me off guard in the hangar. "Growing up here, you learn pretty quick how to weather-proof a room. My first apartment had the worst windows - woke up more than once with snow on my bedroom floor."

The wind rattles the building, and I instinctively step closer to him. Ben's hand finds the small of my back, steady and reassuring.

"We've got enough firewood?" His eyes scan the stack by the fireplace.

"The hotel staff brought up extra before the storm hit." I lean into his touch, just slightly. "They said they've never seen a system move in this fast."

Ben moves to check the fireplace damper, his movements precise and practiced. "Yeah, this one's unusual. Good thing you got those snowshoes earlier. Might need them tomorrow."

I remember my earlier shopping trip, how different the town had felt then - *before* Ben, before this storm, before everything changed. "I'm usually the one making sure everything's secure," I admit. "In the cockpit, I mean. It's strange letting someone else take control."

He pauses in his inspection of the room's heating vent, those bright eyes finding mine. "Trust doesn't come easy to you, does it?"

The question catches me off guard with its insight. "No," I say softly. "It doesn't."

Ben crosses back to me, his steps deliberate. "What about now?"

I look up at him, at this younger man who somehow

makes me feel both protected and exposed. "Now is different."

He cups my face with one hand, thumb brushing my cheek. The tenderness of the gesture nearly undoes me. "Good," he murmurs. "Because I take safety very seriously, Ms. Kramer."

The formality makes me laugh despite myself. "I've noticed, Mr. Huffman."

His other hand settles on my waist as another gust of wind batters the windows. But I barely hear it now, too focused on the warmth of his touch, the steady rise and fall of his chest.

"One more check of the bathroom window," he says, but doesn't move away. "Then we'll be properly secured."

I rest my palm against his chest, feeling his heartbeat through his shirt. "Very thorough."

"Have to be." His voice drops lower. "Precious cargo in here."

The sincerity in his tone steals my breath. I've commanded aircraft through turbulence, navigated storms across continents, but nothing has made me feel as secure as watching this man methodically ensure our safety.

Ben finally steps back, moving toward the bathroom with that same focused determination. I watch him go, admiring the strength in his shoulders, the confidence in his stride. The storm may rage outside, but in here, with him, I've never felt more protected.

Through the bathroom door, I hear him testing the window latch, muttering something about proper insulation. It's such a practical thing, this safety check, but it feels intimate. Personal. Like he's building a shelter just for us.

"Window's good," he calls out.

I hear voices drifting up from downstairs and my pilot instincts kick in immediately. Even off-duty, these passengers are my responsibility. Ben must sense my sudden tension because he heads down to investigate.

The hotel's kitchen feels warmer than it should, probably from all the bodies crowded inside. I recognize Mr. and Mrs. Peterson, the retired teachers from Anchorage, along with Dorothy and Jean, who always book seats together on my flights to visit their grandkids. Thomas Chen, the software engineer who flies this route monthly for work, stands near the industrial coffee maker looking lost.

"We couldn't reach anyone," Dorothy explains, wringing her hands. "The phone lines are down."

"I tried the fire department," Thomas adds, his usual composed demeanor slightly ruffled. "They're dealing with downed power lines all over town. We're not exactly a priority."

I straighten my shoulders, slipping into command mode despite wearing yoga pants and one of Ben's borrowed sweaters. "Alright, let's assess our situation. First priority is making sure everyone's fed."

Ben already has his head in the industrial refrigerator, taking stock. "We've got eggs, cheese, some vegetables. Bread for toast. Should be able to whip up something decent."

"I used to work in a diner," Mrs. Peterson offers, rolling up her sleeves. "Just point me to a spatula."

The kitchen transforms into an impromptu command center, with Ben directing traffic while I organize our volunteers. Dorothy and Jean turn out to be experts at coffee-making, and Thomas proves surprisingly handy with a knife, chopping vegetables for omelets with scientific precision.

"The smell of coffee's going to bring everyone down soon," Ben predicts, methodically cracking eggs into a bowl. He moves with the same focused efficiency I've seen him apply to aircraft engines, and something warm unfurls in my chest watching him take charge alongside me.

Sure enough, the aroma of fresh coffee and sizzling eggs acts like a homing beacon. The rest of my passengers filter in - the college students who'd been sleeping off their holiday parties, the businessman who always books first class, the grandmother traveling to meet her first grandchild. The dining room fills with chatter and the clinking of plates.

I'm placing a fresh pot of coffee on one of the tables when I overhear Mrs. Peterson talking to Ben.

"We always try to book Nora's flights," she's saying, buttering her toast. "Been flying with her for what, three years now? She spotted that mechanical issue last summer before takeoff - saved us all a heap of trouble."

"She's got a sixth sense about these things," Mr. Peterson chimes in. "Most capable pilot we've ever flown with."

Ben's eyes find mine across the room, filled with such naked admiration it makes my breath catch. "I believe it," he says softly. "She's pretty amazing."

The simple sincerity in his voice makes my cheeks warm. Here I am, trapped in a snowstorm with my passengers and a mechanic fifteen years my junior who's somehow managed to completely upend my carefully ordered world in just a few days. And instead of feeling anxious or out of control, I feel... right. Centered. Like all my years of experience and authority aren't at odds with this new, vulnerable part of myself that wants to lean into whatever is building between Ben and me.

Thomas appears at my elbow with another empty coffee carafe. "Captain Kramer? We're running low on filters."

Right. Back to the task at hand. I can sort through my feelings about Ben later. Right now, my passengers need coffee, and that's something I definitely know how to handle.

"There should be a supply closet near the pantry," I say, already moving toward the kitchen. "Let's see what we can find."

Dorothy intercepts me with a plate of eggs. "Eat first, dear. You can't take care of everyone else on an empty stomach."

Ben appears beside me, casually brushing his hand against my lower back as he reaches for the salt. The touch is brief, and professional-looking to anyone watching, but it sends electricity racing along my spine.

"She's right," he murmurs. "Take five minutes to eat. I've got things covered out here."

And he does. I watch him move through the crowd of passengers, refilling coffee cups, checking if anyone needs seconds, fielding questions about the snow removal progress with easy confidence. My passengers respond to him naturally, drawn in by his warm competence and genuine interest in their stories.

"Quite a catch, that young man," Jean comments, sliding into the seat across from me with her own plate. "The way he looks at you reminds me of how my Harold used to look at me, God rest his soul. Age is just a number when you find someone who sees you that clearly."

I almost choke on my eggs, but Jean just pats my hand and returns to her breakfast, leaving me to contemplate how transparent Ben and I apparently are to everyone around us.

The dining room has transformed into an impromptu community space, with passengers sharing stories and passing plates of food. Even the usually reserved businessman is unbent enough to laugh at one of Mr. Peterson's terrible puns. Ben keeps everything running smoothly, anticipating needs before they arise, just like he does with his engines.

I observe all this from my corner seat, professional satisfaction at my passengers' well-being mixing with a deeper, more personal warmth as I watch Ben in his element. He catches my eye occasionally, sharing private smiles that make my heart skip like I'm twenty years younger. When he steps behind me to clear my empty plate, his fingers brush my shoulder in a touch that feels both casual and intimate.

"Your passengers all adore you," he whispers, close enough that I can feel his breath on my ear. "They've been telling me stories about your flights together. If I hadn't already fallen for you completely, hearing about how you handle yourself in the air would have done it."

CHAPTER TEN
half-truths
BEN HUFFMAN

I LEAN against the kitchen counter, watching Nora direct the cleanup efforts with the same precision she probably uses in the cockpit. My chest tightens every time she glances my way, a slight smile playing at her lips. It's hard to believe just hours ago we were...

Focus, Huffman. I shake off the memory and head to the stockroom, flicking on my phone's flashlight to scan the shelves. There's enough dry goods to last maybe three days if we ration carefully. Canned vegetables, pasta, some dried fruit. Not ideal, but we won't starve.

But we can't stay trapped here forever. The thought of being stuck is starting to make my skin crawl, even with the best company I could ask for. Through the tiny stockroom window, all I can see is white. The snow's piled higher than I've ever seen it, and I've lived here my whole life.

When I return to the main room, Nora's deep in conversation with one of the older passengers - Mrs. Henderson, I think her name is. The way Nora leans in, nodding with genuine interest, makes something warm spread through my chest.

That's when it hits me. We can't dig out, but maybe...

I slip into the stairwell, pulling out my phone. Three rings before Liam picks up.

"Finally, you OK? Are you gonna tell me where you are now?"

"Yeah, about that. I'm at the Mountain View B&B. Snowed in with about a dozen other people, including the pilot I was working with."

"You're still with her?" There's a laugh in his voice. "That explains a lot."

"Shut up and listen. I need a favor. You still got contacts with the county plowing crew?"

"Maybe. What's in it for me?"

"How about I don't tell Mom about that time in high school when you—"

"Alright, alright!" He chuckles. "What do you need?"

"Get some guys with plows out here. But come in from the back - parking lot's full of cars we can't move."

"Actually not a bad plan. I'll make some calls."

My relief is short-lived when his tone changes. "But Ben... you should turn on the news. There's another system moving in. A big one."

I press my forehead against the cool wall. "How big?"

"They're saying worse than this one. Marathon's already declared a state of emergency."

"Shit." I glance back toward the main room, where Nora's now helping someone with coffee. "How long do we have?"

"Maybe twelve hours. I'll work fast, get people moving. But Ben..." He pauses. "You might want to prepare everyone for the possibility of a longer stay."

I end the call and just stand there for a moment, processing. Through the stairwell door, I can hear laughter floating up from the kitchen. Nora's voice rises above the others, clear and confident. I should be more worried about being trapped here indefinitely, about the incoming storm, about everything. But something in her voice makes it all feel manageable.

Taking a deep breath, I push off the wall and head back to face whatever's coming. At least I'm not facing it alone.

The kitchen's warmth hits me as I step back in. Nora catches my eye immediately, her expression shifting as she reads something in my face. I try to school my features, but she's already moving toward me.

"Everything okay?" she asks quietly, close enough that her shoulder brushes mine.

"Got hold of my brother," I say, keeping my voice low. "He's going to try to get some plows out here, but..." I glance around at our fellow captives, all busy with their tasks. "We might have another problem heading our way."

Her fingers brush mine, hidden from view by the counter. "Tell me."

I study Nora's face, those keen eyes that seem to read right through me. The words stick in my throat - I should tell her about the incoming storm, about how we might be trapped here far longer than anyone expects. But seeing the way she's finally relaxed, how she's found her footing among these stranded passengers, I can't bring myself to burden her with more worry. Not yet.

"Just some downed power lines blocking the main roads," I say instead, hating how easily the lie comes. "Liam's working on getting the plows redirected, but it might take a day or two to clear everything." I squeeze her hand under the counter, trying to ground myself in the small point of contact. Her skin is warm against mine, and for a moment I almost confess everything. But then Mrs. Henderson calls out about needing help with the coffee maker, and Nora's giving me that small, private smile before turning away. I watch her go, the guilt settling heavy in my stomach alongside the knowledge that I'll have to tell her the truth soon. Just... not yet.

"So we need to be strategic about our supplies," she says when I finish. "And we should probably warn everyone, but carefully. No need to cause panic."

"My thoughts exactly." I resist the urge to take her hand properly. "Liam will do what he can, but..."

"But we should prepare for the worst while hoping for the best." She nods decisively. "Okay. Let me handle the passengers. You double-check everything in the stockroom, make a detailed inventory. We need to know exactly what we're working with."

The professional mask is back in place, but just before she turns away, I catch a flicker of something else in her eyes - trust, maybe. Partnership. Whatever's coming, we'll figure it out together.

I head back to the stockroom, this time with a proper checklist in mind. Behind me, I hear Nora's voice rise slightly as she gathers everyone's attention. Despite everything, there's a small thrill knowing I get to see this side of her - the consummate professional, the natural leader. The woman who, just hours ago, showed me a completely different side of herself.

Focus on the inventory, Huffman. One crisis at a time.

I'm measuring out coffee portions when Thomas Chen corners me by the storage shelves. He's the businessman type - crisp shirt even after being stranded, sharp eyes that miss nothing.

"Mr. Huffman. A moment?" His voice is low, deliberate. "I couldn't help but notice your expression after that phone call. The real situation - how bad is it?"

I hesitate, weighing my options. Thomas strikes me as the steady sort, not prone to panic. Still...

"That obvious, huh?" I run a hand through my hair. "Look, my brother's with emergency services. The news isn't great. There's another system moving in, bigger than this one. They're declaring states of emergency in nearby towns."

Thomas absorbs this with just a slight tightening around his eyes. "Timeline?"

"Twelve hours until it hits. Then potentially 2-4 days of heavy snow."

He nods slowly. "I suspected as much. The barometric pressure readings on my phone have been concerning." He glances toward the main room. "I assume you haven't told Ms. Kramer yet?"

"I was trying to..." The words sound weak even to me. "I didn't want to worry her until we had more information."

"Bad strategy." His tone is matter-of-fact, not accusatory. "She's responsible for those passengers. She needs to know."

The guilt that's been gnawing at me intensifies. "You're right. I know you're right."

"Well, since we're being honest - help me do a proper inventory? Two sets of eyes are better than one."

I grab a notepad, grateful for the distraction. We work methodically through the shelves, Thomas calling out items while I record quantities. His business precision is actually reassuring - there's something comforting about reducing our situation to simple numbers.

"Twenty-eight cans of vegetables, fifteen of fruit. Thirty-two packets of dried soup mix. Eight pounds of pasta..." He pauses at a shelf of baking supplies. "Do you cook?"

"Enough to get by. Nora's better at it."

He raises an eyebrow at my casual use of her first name but doesn't comment. "With careful rationing, we could stretch this to a week. Maybe more if—"

"Ben?"

Nora's voice makes me jump. She's standing in the doorway, arms crossed, expression unreadable. "Can we talk? Alone?"

Thomas gives me a pointed look as he slides past her. "I'll finish the count later."

The stockroom feels smaller once it's just the two of us. Nora closes the door, and my stomach drops at her expression.

"What did Liam really tell you?" Her voice is quiet but firm. "And don't even think about sugar-coating it this time."

I meet her eyes, seeing the hurt beneath the professional mask. "There's another storm coming. A big one. Marathon's already declared a state of emergency." The words tumble out in a rush. "They're saying it could snow for another two to four days straight."

She doesn't react immediately, just processes the information with the same focus she gives to flight calculations. "When were you planning to tell me this?"

"I was going to. Soon. I just..." I step closer, fighting the urge to reach for her. "You seemed so relieved earlier, having found your groove with everyone. I didn't want to add more pressure."

"That wasn't your call to make." Her words sting because they're true. "I'm not some delicate flower you need to protect, Ben. I'm the captain of this group, stranded or not. I need all the information to make proper decisions."

"You're right. I'm sorry." I lean against a shelf, suddenly exhausted. "I screwed up. Thomas already read me the riot act about it."

"Thomas?" Her eyebrows lift. "Is that why you two were huddled in here?"

"He figured it out on his own. We were doing inventory, trying to calculate how long we can stretch our supplies."

Something in her expression softens slightly. "And?"

"With careful rationing, maybe a week. Thomas thinks we might be able to extend it further if we're smart about it."

Nora nods, already shifting into problem-solving mode. "Okay. First, you're going to tell me everything Liam said - every detail. Then we're going to gather everyone and lay out the situation. No more secrets, no more protecting me. Clear?"

"Crystal." I risk a small smile. "Does this mean I'm forgiven?"

"That depends." She steps closer, voice dropping. "Are you done trying to handle me?"

"Completely done. You're clearly better at handling things than I am anyway."

"Don't forget it." Her fingers brush mine briefly. "Now, tell me everything, starting with that phone call."

CHAPTER ELEVEN
soft blankets
NORA KRAMER

I STAND before my gathered passengers in the dining room, their faces a mix of concern and resignation. The weight of responsibility settles heavy on my shoulders as I deliver the news about the second storm heading our way.

"Everyone, please remain calm. We're monitoring the situation closely. For your safety, I need you all to stay in your rooms until further notice." My pilot's voice comes through - steady, authoritative.

Ben steps forward, his presence beside me reassuring. "The generators are holding up for now, but I want to be honest - we can't guarantee they'll keep running indefinitely." His frankness, something I'm growing to love about him, cuts through any false hopes.

In the corner, Thomas perks up when Ben mentions needing help with the firewood situation. The engineer's eyes light up at the mention of dismantling chairs for fuel.

"I've got some ideas about maximizing our wood supply," Thomas says, already pulling out a small notebook. "If we cut them at specific angles, we can ensure each room gets adequate heat."

I watch Ben work the room, moving from person to person, answering questions, offering reassurance. He's a natural leader in crisis, something I never expected from our first meeting at the hangar. My chest tightens with pride and something deeper.

When the last passenger heads upstairs, I let out a long breath. "I don't know what I would've done without you here." The words come out softer than intended.

Ben turns to me, snowflakes melting in his dark hair from his last trip outside. "You'd have figured it out. You're the most capable person I know."

"Flying a plane is one thing. This…" I gesture around us. "This is completely different."

BACK IN OUR ROOM, Ben builds a fire while I check the satellite phone one last time. No signal. I wonder if Sarah is OK.

The flames catch quickly, casting dancing shadows across the walls. I sink into the couch beside him, watching his profile in the firelight.

I curl deeper into the couch, watching the flames dance while Ben's arm wraps around my shoulders. The warmth from the fire mingles with his body heat, creating a cocoon of comfort I haven't experienced in... I can't even remember how long.

"What's going on in that head of yours?" Ben's voice rumbles against my ear.

I trace idle patterns on his forearm, considering how to put these feelings into words. My usual precise, measured way of speaking feels inadequate. "I'm thinking about how strange life is. A week ago, I was furious about being grounded here. Now..."

He waits, patient as always, giving me space to sort through my thoughts. That's another thing about him - he never rushes me, never tries to fill the silence.

"Now I'm wondering how I got so lucky," I admit

quietly. The words feel dangerous, like opening an airlock mid-flight. But they're true.

My last relationship with Marcus had been all sharp edges and careful negotiations. Everything calculated, scheduled, proper. Perfect on paper - both of us career-focused professionals who understood the demands of our jobs. But there was never this... ease.

Ben shifts slightly, his fingers playing with the ends of my hair. Such a simple gesture, yet it sends shivers down my spine. "You know what I love about you?" he asks.

The word 'love' hangs in the air between us. My heart stutters.

"What?" I manage to ask.

"How you can command a room full of nervous passengers one minute, then curl up like a cat the next. You contain multitudes, Nora Kramer."

I laugh softly, but my mind is spinning. Love. He said love so casually, so naturally. And instead of setting off warning bells like it should - like it always has before - it feels right.

The realization hits me like clear-air turbulence: I'm falling in love with him. No, that's not quite right. I've already fallen.

I sit up straighter, look into his eyes. They're warm, steady, holding mine without hesitation. None of my usual cautionary voices are chiming in - no warnings about age differences or career complications or what others might think. For once, those voices are completely silent.

"Ben..." I start, then pause. How do you tell someone they've completely upended your carefully ordered world in the best possible way?

He reaches up, traces my cheekbone with his thumb. "You don't have to say anything."

But I want to. I need to. "I've never felt like this before," I confess. "This comfortable. This... myself."

The fire pops, sending sparks up the chimney. Outside, the wind howls, reminding us of the storm that brought us together. But in here, in this moment, everything is still and perfect.

"I keep waiting for it to feel wrong," I continue, the words flowing now. "For all the reasons it should feel wrong to kick in. The age gap, our different lives, the fact that we met because my plane broke down. But it doesn't. Being with you feels like..." I search for the right analogy. "Like breaking through cloud cover into clear skies."

Ben's smile spreads slowly, reaching his eyes. "That might be the most romantic thing anyone's ever said to me, especially coming from you."

"What's that supposed to mean?" I arch an eyebrow.

"Just that you're usually so precise, so technical. Hearing you wax poetic... it's nice."

I feel my cheeks warm. "Don't get used to it."

He pulls me closer, and I melt against him. "Too late. I'm already used to you."

The simple statement hits me right in the chest. Because I'm used to him too. Used to his laugh, his thoughtfulness, the way he hums while he works. Used to the way he looks at me like I'm something precious but not fragile. Used to the feeling of his hand in mine, the sound of his breathing as he sleeps.

Love. The word echoes in my mind again. It should terrify me. Instead, it feels like coming home.

A log shifts in the fireplace, sending up another shower of sparks. Ben gets up to tend to it, and I watch him move, the sure efficiency of his movements, the strength in his shoulders. When did I memorize the way he moves? When did my heart start recognizing his presence before my eyes do?

He settles back beside me, and I immediately seek his warmth again. His arm comes around me automatically, like we've been doing this for years instead of days.

"Tell me what you're thinking now," he murmurs into my hair.

I close my eyes, breathing in his scent - a mix of wood smoke and something uniquely him. "I'm thinking that I don't want this storm to end," I admit. "Is that terrible?"

His chest rumbles with quiet laughter. "If it is, then I'm terrible too."

The wind rattles the windows, but inside our bubble of warmth, nothing can touch us. "I need to tell you something," I say, my heart racing. "These past few days, stuck here with you... I've never felt more alive. More myself." I take a deep breath. "I think I'm falling in love with you."

Ben's hands still on my arm, his eyes reflecting the firelight. "I've been in love with you since that sunset view."

The last patch of visible window slowly disappears under fresh snow as he pulls me closer. His kiss is gentle at first, then deepens with urgency. My fingers trace the muscles of his back through his shirt as he lowers me onto the couch.

The fire crackles beside us as clothing falls away. His touch ignites something primal in me, making me forget about the storm, the stranded passengers, the age difference - everything except the feel of his skin against mine.

"You're beautiful," he whispers against my neck, his hands exploring every curve.

I arch into his touch, gasping as he finds sensitive spots. The cold outside makes his warmth even more intoxicating. We move together slowly at first, savoring each sensation, each kiss, each shared breath.

The storm howls outside our window, but inside this room, we've created our own perfect shelter. His body covers mine completely as we rock together, the fire's warmth nothing compared to the heat building between us.

When release comes, it's like flying through clear skies - that moment of perfect freedom and weightlessness. Ben holds me close afterward, our breathing gradually slowing, syncing with the rhythm of the falling snow outside.

Wrapped in a soft blanket, I nestle against Ben's chest on the couch, listening to his steady heartbeat. The fire casts a warm glow across our bare skin as snowflakes continue their relentless dance outside. His fingers trace lazy patterns on my shoulder, and I've never felt more at peace.

"Tell me about where you grew up," I murmur, playing with his fingers.

Here's a rewritten version of those sentences:

"Small town way up here in Alaska," Ben says, his voice deep and resonant. "My dad owned the only auto shop in town, so I was practically raised with grease under my fingernails."

"Is that where you learned to fix planes?"

"Yeah, I started out with crop dusters. The local farmers needed someone to keep their old machines running." He chuckles, a sound that resonates within me. "What about you?"

"Boston girl, born and raised. Dad was in the Air Force, mom ran an art gallery." I smile at the memory. "They thought I was crazy when I announced I wanted to be a pilot instead of following mom into academia."

Ben pulls me closer. "What made you choose flying?"

"Freedom. The first time I went up in a small Cessna, I knew nothing else would ever compare." I trace the line of his collarbone. "Well, almost nothing."

"Where's the best place you've ever flown?" His voice holds genuine curiosity.

"That's tough." I shift to look at him. "Alaska's raw beauty is incredible - the glaciers, the northern lights. But there's this tiny airport in the Caribbean, on St. Barts. The runway ends right at the beach. You're descending over turquoise water one moment, then touching down the next. The contrast is stunning - from ice and snow to palm trees and white sand."

"I'd love to see that someday." His words hold promise.

"What about you? Any serious relationships before?" I ask, trying to keep my voice casual.

"Two." Ben's hand continues its gentle exploration of my skin. "Jodi in tech school - typical first love stuff. Then Paulina, a flight attendant who flew in last summer. A fling, mostly. I couldn't leave my work here."

I nod, understanding the pull of place and purpose.

"Your turn," he prompts softly.

"David was my college sweetheart. We tried making it work while I was in flight school, but the distance killed it." I pause, remembering. "Then Marcus, another pilot. That lasted three years until we realized we were more in love with flying than each other."

"And now?" Ben's question hangs in the air.

I prop myself up on one elbow, meeting his gaze. "Now I'm here with someone who makes me forget about age, about what others might think. Someone who sees me, not just the uniform."

Ben cups my face in his hand, thumb brushing my cheek. "You know what amazes me about you? How you command respect without demanding it. The way you handled everything today with the passengers - that wasn't just training. That was pure you."

"You're not so bad yourself," I smile, leaning into his touch. "The way you connect with people, make them feel heard... it's beautiful to watch."

He pulls me down for a kiss that starts gentle but quickly deepens. My hands slide into his hair as his grip tightens on my waist. The blanket slips, but the fire's warmth and our shared body heat keep the cold at bay.

"I never expected this," I whisper against his lips. "You've completely upended my world."

"In a good way?" His eyes search mine.

"In the best way." I settle back against his chest, listening to the wood crackle in the fireplace. "Tell me more about what little Ben was like?"

His laughter rumbles through both of us as he launches into stories about his first attempts at fixing engines, childhood adventures with his brother, and the time he accidentally set his dad's workshop on fire trying to build a rocket.

I share my own memories - sneaking onto the roof of our brownstone to watch planes, my first solo flight, the feeling of breaking through clouds into endless blue sky.

As we talk, our hands continue their gentle exploration, learning each other's bodies in the firelight. Every touch, every shared story brings us closer, building something deeper than physical attraction.

CHAPTER TWELVE
saved by a tractor
BEN HUFFMAN

I WAKE up feeling more rested than I have in years, maybe ever. My body feels light, relaxed in a way that's completely foreign to me. Usually, I'm up before dawn, muscles already tensing for another day of wrestling with engines and metal. But this morning? This morning is different.

Nora's curled against me, her breathing deep and steady. Her dark hair fans across the pillow, and I hold my breath, not wanting to disturb this moment. Not wanting to wake her. The steady rise and fall of her chest hypnotize me, and I find myself matching my breathing to hers.

My phone's on the nightstand, and I carefully stretch to grab it, moving with the stealth of someone defusing a bomb. 9 A.M. Shit. I never sleep this late. Never. But then again, I've never been snowed in at a B&B with a gorgeous pilot who somehow sees past the age gap and my grease-monkey exterior.

The window's completely covered in white, not even a hint of daylight seeping through. Last night's storm was brutal - I can still hear the echo of those winds in my head. The whole building shook with each gust, windows rattling like they might give in at any moment. Nora had pressed closer to me with each blast, though she'd never admit being rattled by something as mundane as the weather.

I squint at the windowpane, trying to gauge how much snow we got. The glass is completely obscured, which isn't a good sign. If it's piled that high on the vertical surface... Christ, the roof! My mind starts running calculations - snow load ratings, structural integrity, the age of this building. The engineer in me can't help it.

My free hand reaches for my phone again, this time to check for messages from Liam. Nothing. The signal bars flicker between one and zero - not surprising given the weather. I should be more worried about being trapped here, about the passengers downstairs, about the logistics of getting everyone out safely. But with Nora's warmth pressed against me, her head tucked perfectly under my chin, it's hard to feel anything but content.

I trace patterns on her shoulder with my fingertips, marveling at how smooth her skin is. *How did I get here?* A week ago I was just another small-town mechanic, content with my routine of engines and solitude. Now I'm tangled up with this incredible woman who commands the skies, who carries herself with such authority and grace that she makes me forget the fifteen years between us.

The building creaks ominously, and I strain my ears trying to identify where the sound came from. Above us? Beside us? The engineer in me wants to investigate, to assess the situation, but moving means disturbing Nora. Means breaking this bubble we're in.

Through the wall, I hear muffled voices - probably the other guests stirring. Soon we'll have to face reality again. Deal with the storm, the stranded passengers, the dwindling supplies. But for now, I let myself sink deeper into the mattress, breathing in the scent of Nora's hair.

My mind drifts to last night - how her face looked in the firelight, how her voice softened when she told me she loved me too. It still doesn't feel real. Like maybe this is all some elaborate dream brought on by too many hours under aircraft engines, breathing in fuel fumes.

Another violent gust rocks the building, and this time the rattle is accompanied by a deep groaning sound from above. That can't be good. My muscles tense involuntarily as my mind starts cataloging everything that could go wrong with this much snow load. The age of the building, the likely construction methods used when it was built, the accumulated weight of hour after hour of heavy snowfall...

I glance at the ceiling, noting hairline cracks I hadn't seen before. Are they new? Or am I just being paranoid? The practical part of my brain is screaming at me to get up, to check the structure, to make sure everyone's safe. But Nora shifts against me, mumbling something in her sleep, and I'm frozen in place.

Her hand rests on my chest, right over my heart, and I wonder if she can feel it beating faster as my concerns about the building mount. I should wake her. Should tell her about my worries regarding the structural integrity. But she's been under so much stress already, dealing with the grounded plane, the stranded passengers, the storm...

The wind howls again, a sound that seems to come from everywhere and nowhere at once. The windows shudder in their frames, and I swear I can feel the floor vibrate beneath us. Or maybe that's just my imagination running wild. Years of fixing things have taught me to expect the worst, to look for problems before they become catastrophes.

I jolt sitting up to the distinctive rumble of engines and muffled shouts cutting through the morning silence. The mechanical sounds grow louder, and my heart races as I recognize the distinct whine of snowplows.

"That's Liam," I say, jumping out of bed. "He actually did it."

"What?" Nora sits up, pulling the blanket around her. The fire we built last night has died down to embers.

"My brother. I called him yesterday, asked him to bring help." I'm already pulling on my jeans and searching for my shirt. "He must have rounded up the guys from the shop."

Nora moves with the swift efficiency I've come to admire, transforming from my sleeping companion to a capable pilot in moments. "We need to alert the passengers."

"I'll check the back entrance, make sure it's them." I pause to kiss her quickly, still amazed that I can do that now.

We hurry downstairs, our footsteps echoing in the empty breakfast area. The generators have kept the lights on, but the windows are completely blocked by snow, creating an eerie artificial atmosphere.

"I'll start knocking on doors," Nora says, already heading for the stairs. Her voice carries that natural authority as she calls out in the hallways: "Everyone please come downstairs! Rescue crews have arrived!"

I hear doors opening above, voices rising with hope and relief. The first guests appear on the stairs as I clear the stored chairs away from the back door. Mrs. Henderson, the elderly passenger who helped us cook yesterday, gives me a knowing smile as she settles at one of the tables.

More passengers filter in, some still in their pajamas with coats hastily thrown over them. The breakfast area fills with excited chatter, a stark contrast to yesterday's worried silence. I keep glancing at Nora, watching her move among her passengers with that perfect blend of professional care and personal warmth.

The mechanical sounds grow closer until they're right outside. Then comes the knock we've been waiting for - three sharp raps on the storage area door.

"Stand back, everyone," I call out, moving to unlock it. The door swings open, and there's Liam, grinning like he just won the lottery. Behind him, I can see the pathway they've carved through the snow - walls of white rising easily fifteen feet on either side.

"Holy shit," I breathe, taking in the scale of what we've been trapped in.

"That's what I said." Liam pulls me into a bear hug. "You sure know how to pick your shelter-in-place locations, little brother."

When we break apart, I turn to find Nora standing nearby. "This is—"

"Nora Kramer," she says, extending her hand to Liam. "Your brother's been invaluable during this whole ordeal."

"Has he now?" Liam's eyes dance with amusement as he shakes her hand, and I know I'm in for some serious questioning later.

The passengers start filing past us, exclaiming at the snow walls and thanking Liam and his crew profusely. I count four snowplows and at least six guys I recognize from around town, all looking tired but pleased with their rescue operation.

Mrs. Henderson stops to pat my cheek as she passes. "Such a nice young man," she says, loud enough for both

Nora and Liam to hear. "You take care of our pilot, now."

I feel my face heat up, but when I glance at Nora, she's trying to hide a smile. Liam looks between us, his eyebrows climbing higher by the second.

"Everyone," Nora speaks up. "Go back to your rooms and pack up your suitcases, we're going home!"

"The crews have cleared a path to the main road," Liam announces as well. "We've got vehicles waiting to transport everyone to the community center. They've set up a temporary shelter there until the roads are completely cleared."

The relief in the air is tangible as our little group of stranded travelers makes their way back into the B&B to pack their things. I hang back with Nora, watching our unlikely family disperse.

"Ben," Liam calls out, "you riding with me or...?" He leaves the question hanging, his eyes flicking to Nora.

Before I can respond, Nora threads her fingers through mine. "I think he's with me," she says, and the certainty in her voice makes my heart skip.

Liam's grin threatens to split his face. "Yeah, I figured as much." He turns to join the rescue crew, but not before shooting me a thumbs-up behind Nora's back.

We stand in the doorway of our snow cave shelter, watching the procession of people and vehicles. Nora's hand is warm in mine, and despite the chaos of the rescue operation, this moment feels strangely peaceful.

"You called your brother to save us," she says softly.

"Well, I couldn't let you miss too many flights. Bad for business."

She bumps my shoulder with hers. "My hero."

"Does this mean I get a proper date when we're out of here? One without a natural disaster involved?"

"I think that can be arranged." She squeezes my hand. "Though I have to admit, the natural disaster worked out pretty well for us."

CHAPTER THIRTEEN
love or lust?
NORA KRAMER

THROUGH THE WINDOW of my temporary office at the small regional airport, I watch the transformed landscape of this Alaskan town. Several feet of pristine snow blanket everything in sight, creating an otherworldly scene that's both beautiful and daunting. The steady rumble of snowplows has become the town's heartbeat, their orange frames moving methodically through the streets day and night like determined Worker bees.

"Another cup?" Ben appears in my doorway, holding two steaming mugs.

My heart skips. Even after a week, he still has this effect on me. "Thanks."

Outside, the town exists in a strange duality – chaos and serenity intertwined. Residents shovel their driveways with practiced efficiency while children build towering snowmen. The plows push enormous walls of snow to the sides of the streets, creating miniature mountain ranges along the sidewalks. Emergency vehicles still race through occasionally, their sirens muffled by the snow-dampened air.

"The roads to the hangar are finally clear," Ben says, leaning against my desk. "I should have the plane ready by tomorrow afternoon."

The words hit me harder than expected. Tomorrow. My stomach tightens as I watch him walk over to the window, his profile strong against the bright snow-reflected light. In the hangar, I can see his team working on my aircraft, their movements precise and purposeful as the snow continues melting around them, creating silvery rivulets down the building's sides.

"I have to take them home, Ben." The words feel heavy in my mouth. "Those passengers trusted me to get them to their destination."

He turns, and the pain in his eyes makes my chest ache. "Let someone else fly them. Sarah could—"

"You know I can't do that." I stand up, needing to move, to do something with this restless energy. "It's my responsibility."

"Nora." He catches my hand as I pass, his touch sending that familiar warmth through me. "If you leave... I can't shake this feeling I'll never see you again."

"Don't say that." I squeeze his fingers, trying to convince us both. "I'll come back. I promise."

But the uncertainty hangs between us like fog, thick and obscuring.

THE NEXT DAY comes too quickly. In the cockpit, I run through my pre-flight checks with mechanical precision, trying to focus on the familiar routine rather than the ache in my chest. The passengers file in, their cheerful voices carrying forward as they find their seats. They're happy to finally be heading home, and I should be happy too.

"Ready, Captain?" Sarah slides into the co-pilot seat beside me, her expression carefully neutral.

I nod, unable to trust my voice just yet. Through the

windshield, I can see Ben standing at the edge of the tarmac, his hands stuffed in his pockets, watching.

Once we're airborne and cruising at altitude, Sarah turns to me. "Alright, spill it. What's really going on with you and the mechanic?"

The question I've been dreading. I keep my eyes fixed on the instruments, but the truth spills out anyway. "I think I'm in love with him."

Sarah's laugh is sharp and unexpected. "Oh honey, no."

"Yes," I say quickly.

"No," she replies quickly.

"Yes."

Sarah laughs, "That's not *love* – that's what happens when you throw two attractive people together in a crisis situation."

"It's not like that—"

"It's *exactly* like that." Her voice softens with practiced wisdom. "It's close proximity sex. When you're stuck together, emotions run high, adrenaline's pumping... it feels intense and real, but it's just lust dressed up as something bigger."

I want to argue, to defend what Ben and I shared, but doubt creeps in like a slow frost. *Was she right? Had I mistaken physical attraction and unusual circumstances for something deeper?*

"Think about it," Sarah continues. "You barely know him. A week ago, he was just the mechanic called to fix our plane. Now suddenly you're in love? That's not how real relationships work."

The altitude indicators blur slightly as I blink hard. "But it felt—"

"Real? Of course it did. That's how *lust* works. It's powerful and immediate and makes you think you've found your soulmate." She pats my arm. "Trust me, once you're back home and in your normal routine, these feelings will fade faster than that snow we left behind."

I stare out at the endless sky, trying to sort through the tumult in my chest. Every moment with Ben plays through my mind like a highlight reel – his laugh, his touch, the way he took charge during the storm, how safe I felt in his arms. But now Sarah's words cast shadows over each memory, making me question everything I thought I knew.

Was it all just an illusion created by extraordinary circumstances? Had I let myself get carried away by physical attraction and the romance of being stranded together? The certainty I felt just hours ago begins to crumble like snow under warm rain.

The worst part is that Sarah's logic makes sense. Too much sense. In my normal life – the life I'm flying back to – would there really be room for a relationship with a younger mechanic from a small Alaskan town? Had I been fooling myself all along?

I adjust our heading slightly, the familiar action offering no comfort. Because now I'm left wondering if I made the right choice in leaving, or if I'm running away from something real because it's easier to believe it was never real at all.

I PUSH open my front door, and the emptiness hits me like a physical force. The house is dark and still, exactly as I left it two weeks ago. My suitcase wheels echo against the hardwood as I drag it inside, the sound amplified in the silence.

"Home sweet home," I mutter, but the words feel hollow.

Everything is precisely where I left it - the stack of aviation magazines on the coffee table, my favorite throw draped over the armchair, even the coffee mug I'd hurriedly rinsed and left to dry by the sink. Yet somehow, it all feels different. Or maybe I'm the one who's different.

I climb the stairs slowly, each step taking more effort than it should. My bedroom is bathed in the soft glow of city lights filtering through the windows. I don't bother turning on the lamp. Instead, I drop my bags and walk straight to the balcony - my favorite spot in the house.

I walk towards the railing and Seattle spreads out below me, a glittering tapestry of lights and shadows. In the distance, I can see the familiar pattern of runway lights at Sea-Tac, planes descending and ascending in their choreographed dance. *How many times have I stood here, finding comfort in that view?* It was one of the main reasons I bought this house - being able to see my sanctuary, my refuge, from my own bedroom balcony.

But tonight, watching those planes doesn't bring the usual sense of peace. Instead, my mind keeps drifting back to a small Alaskan hangar, to strong hands confidently working on engine parts, to blue eyes that crinkled at the corners when they smiled.

"It wasn't just lust," I whisper to my reflection in the window. Sarah's words from the flight echo in my head, but they ring false against the memory of Ben's touch, his laugh, the way he looked at me like I was something precious.

Lust doesn't explain the way my heart settled when he was near. It doesn't explain how natural it felt to work alongside him in that B&B kitchen, or how we could talk for hours about everything and nothing. Lust doesn't account for the way he knew exactly what I needed before I did - whether it was a cup of coffee or just a quiet moment of understanding.

I feel a headache coming on and I pinch my fingers on the bridge of my nose. Below, a plane's landing lights pierce through the night as it descends toward the runway. Usually, that sight fills me with anticipation, with the promise of new horizons. Now it just reminds me of what - *who* - I left behind.

The lights of Seattle twinkle mockingly. This view used to make me feel connected to everything I loved about my life. Now it just emphasizes how alone I am. My sanctuary has become a reminder of what's missing.

I turn around and head back to my bedroom. I wrap my arms around myself, feeling the phantom warmth of Ben's embrace. In Alaska, even in the midst of a snowstorm, I'd never felt cold. Now, standing in my climate-controlled bedroom, I can't seem to get warm.

My phone sits heavy in my pocket. I could call him. His number is still there, though I haven't had the courage to use it since I left. *What would I even say?* 'I miss you'? 'I made a mistake'? 'I'm standing here looking at planes and wishing they were flying me back to you instead of away'?

The city lights blur as tears fill my eyes. My perfect view of the airport - the view I'd fallen in love with, the view I'd paid a premium for - suddenly feels like a cruel joke. What good is watching planes take off and land when the one person I want to fly to is hundreds of miles away?

I turn away from the window, but I can still see the runway lights reflecting off the walls. My sanctuary has become a prison of my own making, and I don't know how to break free. The airfield that once represented endless possibilities now only shows me the distance between where I am and where my heart wants to be.

CHAPTER FOURTEEN
a fool who fell too hard

BEN HUFFMAN

I STARE at my phone again, checking for any messages from Nora. Nothing. The screen mocks me with its emptiness, just like it has for the past week. My stomach churns as I remember our last moments together - her promises to return, the warmth in her eyes, the way she held onto me before climbing into that cockpit.

The tracking system at our small tower confirmed she made it safely to her destination. At least there's that. But since then?

Radio silence.

I slam my wrench down harder than necessary, making Diego jump at the workbench beside me. The metallic clang echoes through the hangar, matching the hollow feeling in my chest.

"Sorry," I mutter, running a hand through my hair. "Just... distracted."

"Woman troubles?" Diego raises an eyebrow, not looking up from the carburetor he's cleaning.

I grunt in response, picking up the wrench again. Woman troubles. Yeah, that's one way to put it. My mind drifts to Jodi, my first serious girlfriend back in college. The tears in her eyes when I told her I needed space, that I wasn't ready for the future she was planning. "You're choosing your career over me," she'd accused. And she was right.

Then there was Paulina last year. Another relationship I'd ended, another heart I'd broken because I couldn't give her what she wanted. "You're emotionally unavailable," she'd said, hurling the words like weapons. At the time, I'd defended myself, and argued that I just needed to focus on building my business.

Now? Now I get it. The universe has a sick sense of humor, making me feel exactly what I put *them* through.

"You look like someone killed your dog," Diego comments, breaking into my thoughts.

"Feels worse." The admission slips out before I can stop it. I've never been one to talk about feelings, especially not at work, but this ache in my chest won't go away. Every time I walk past a private jet I'm reminded about the one she flew in on, every time I smell that fancy coffee from the café where we had breakfast, every time I see snow starting to fall - it's like someone's twisting a knife in my gut.

I pull out my phone again, knowing nothing's changed in the last twenty minutes. No messages. No calls. No explanation.

"You know what's really messed up?" I say, more to myself than Diego. "When I ended things with Jodi and Paulina, I told myself it was because I hadn't found the right person. That when I met someone special enough, I'd know. I'd feel it."

Diego sets down his tools, finally giving me his full attention.

"And now?" He prompts.

"Now I found that person. Someone who gets me, who understands the passion I have for this work because she has it too. Someone who challenges me, who makes me laugh, who sees past the age difference and just sees... me." My voice cracks slightly. "And she's gone."

The irony isn't lost on me. All those times I was the one walking away, convinced I was doing the right thing, telling myself they'd get over it. Was this how Jodi felt when I stopped returning her calls? How Paulina felt when I said I needed to focus on my career?

This hollow feeling in my chest, like someone scooped out everything that mattered and left nothing but an echo chamber for my regrets - is this what heartbreak feels like?

I pick up a rag and mindlessly wipe grease from my hands, trying to focus on the familiar motion instead of the memories flooding my mind. That night during the snowstorm, watching her sleep beside me. The way she'd curl into me, trusting and vulnerable in a way that made my chest tight. How she looked in the morning light, her guard down, just being herself.

"You tried calling her?" Diego asks, breaking into my thoughts again.

"Yeah." I toss the rag aside with more force than necessary. "Left messages. Sent texts. Nothing."

The age difference must have finally hit home once she was back in her normal life.

I've always prided myself on being self-sufficient, on not needing anyone. Hell, that's partly why I ended things with Jodi and Paulina - I couldn't handle their need for me, their expectations. But now? Now I understand that desperate feeling, that ache to hear someone's voice, to know they're thinking about you too.

"The worst part?" I continue, barely registering that I'm still talking out loud. "I keep thinking about all the things I should have said. Should have done. Should have made her understand that this wasn't just some snowstorm fling for me. That I've never felt this way about anyone."

Diego whistles low. "You got it bad, hermano."

"Yeah." I pick up my wrench again, needing to do something with my hands. "I do."

The metal is cold against my palm, and I remember how warm her hand felt in mine as we watched the snowfall. How right it felt. How complete. Now everything feels off-kilter like I'm walking around with a crucial piece missing.

Is this karma? The universe's way of teaching me a lesson about all those hearts I broke? Because if it is, message received. Loud and clear. This hollow ache, this constant checking of my phone, this analysis of every moment we shared, wondering what I could have done differently - it's a special kind of torture.

Liam's heavy footsteps echo across the hangar floor. I quickly pocket my phone and grab a wrench, pretending to be absorbed in the engine repair before me.

One look was all it took.

"Still nothing?" His voice carries that mixture of concern and judgment I've grown to hate.

"She's probably just busy." The words sound hollow even to my own ears.

Liam leans against the workbench, arms crossed. "Think it's time we had a real talk, little brother."

"If this is about Nora—"

"It is." He cuts me off. "Look, I've seen this before. Older woman, trapped situation—a young guy who's eager to please..."

My grip tightens on the wrench. "Don't."

"She needed warmth during a storm, Ben. Someone to make her feel good, feel young again. It's a tale as old as time."

"You don't know her," I snap, but doubt starts creeping in like frost around the edges of my certainty. "Nora's different."

"Is she? Then why hasn't she called? Texted? Given any sign that what happened meant something more than a convenient distraction?"

I want to argue, but memories start shifting in my mind. The way she hesitated before our first kiss. Her initial reluctance to let things progress. Had I seen what I wanted to see, rather than what was really there?

"She told me she loved me," I say, but my voice wavers.

"In the middle of a snowstorm, trapped together, emotions running high..." Liam shakes his head. "People say lots of things in moments like that."

I drop the wrench with a clang and pull out my phone again. My fingers hover over her number. "I should call her."

"Ben—"

I hit dial anyway, turning away from Liam's disapproving look. The phone rings once before clicking over to voicemail. Her professional greeting feels like a slap in the face.

"Hey, it's me. Again." I pause, hating how desperate I sound. "Just wanted to make sure you got home okay. Call me when you can."

I hang up and stare at the phone, willing it to ring. Instead, I type out a quick text:

> Missing you Hope everything's alright

Minutes tick by. No response. No read receipt. Nothing.

The doubt Liam planted grows larger, feeding on my insecurities. Maybe he's right. Maybe I was just a convenient distraction, a way to pass time during an unexpected layover. The thought makes me feel cheap, used.

I grab my tools and head to the next repair job. Work has always been my escape, my constant. At least engines make sense - when something's broken, you can diagnose the problem, fix it, move on. Not like matters of the heart, where everything is messy and unclear.

The afternoon stretches on as I lose myself in the familiar rhythm of repairs. Every few minutes, I check my phone, but the screen remains stubbornly blank.

No messages.

No calls.

No Nora.

My brother's words echo in my head: "People say lots of things in moments like that." Had I misread everything? The connection I felt, the way she looked at me, the vulnerable conversations we shared - was it all just part of getting through the storm?

The metal tool in my hand grows slick with sweat as these thoughts tumble through my mind. I've had relationships before, but nothing that felt like this. Nothing that made me question my own judgment so completely.

I check my phone one more time. Still nothing. The message I sent sits there, unread, like a testament to my naivety. I want to believe she's just busy, that there's a reasonable explanation for her silence. But with each passing hour, that belief gets harder to maintain.

The sun starts setting outside the hangar windows, casting long shadows across the concrete floor.

Another day without a word from her.

Another day of feeling like a fool who fell too hard, too fast.

What a fucking idiot I am...

CHAPTER FIFTEEN

play the game

BEN HUFFMAN

TWO WEEKS of silence feels like two years. Every morning, I check my phone, hoping to see her name light up the screen. Nothing. The empty notifications mock me, each one a reminder of what I've lost - or maybe what I never really had.

I throw myself into work, but even the familiar comfort of engines and metal can't dull the ache.

My hands move through the familiar motions of a plane's engine, but my mind keeps drifting. Two weeks. No call, no text, nothing. The socket wrench slips, and I curse under my breath.

"Earth to Ben." Diego's voice cuts through my brooding. He's leaning against the workbench, arms crossed, wearing that knowing look I've come to hate. "That's the third time you've retightened the same bolt."

"Just being thorough." I wipe my hands on a shop rag, trying to look busy.

"Right." He shuffles through some paperwork. "Well, if you're done being 'thorough,' we've got three oil changes waiting, and the Henderson kid's motorcycle needs a new timing belt."

I nod, grateful for the distraction. "How's that transmission rebuild coming along?"

"Finished it yesterday while you were…" He pauses, choosing his words carefully. "Taking your lunch break at the airport."

Heat creeps up my neck. I've been transparent, spending my breaks watching planes take off, scanning the sky like some lovesick teenager. "Just checking on parts delivery."

"Sure, jefe." Diego's expression softens. "Look, everything's running smooth here. Maybe take the afternoon, clear your head?"

I start to protest, but he's right. I'm no good to anyone like this. "Thanks, man. I'll make it up to you."

The drive through town feels different now. Every street corner holds a memory - the café where we had breakfast, the lookout point where we almost kissed. Even the damn grocery store reminds me of her laughing at my terrible jokes about frozen dinners.

I spot Liam's truck parked near the highway crew, its familiar dents and scratches visible even from here. The remaining snow banks are finally starting to look manageable, more like speed bumps than walls. I pull over, killing the engine.

Liam sees me coming and hops down from his perch in the plow. "Taking a break from pining?" He's trying for humor, but I hear the concern underneath.

"Funny. How's the cleanup going?"

He shrugs, gesturing at the cleared lanes. "Almost back to normal. Another week, maybe less." He studies my face. "You look like shit."

"Thanks for the update." I kick at a chunk of dirty snow. "Got everything under control here?"

"Yeah, we're good." He hesitates. "Listen, Ben—"

"Don't." I hold up a hand. "I know what you're going to say."

"Do you? Because from where I'm standing, you're torturing yourself over someone who made her choice pretty clear."

The truth in his words stings, but I'm not ready to hear it. Not yet. "I should get back to the shop."

"Ben." Liam's voice stops me. "You're my little brother. I hate seeing you like this."

"I'm fine." The lie tastes bitter. "Just busy with work."

"Right." He doesn't believe me, but he lets it drop. "Come by for dinner tonight? Mom's making that pasta thing you like."

"Maybe." We both know I won't. I've been avoiding family dinners, tired of the concerned looks and careful conversations.

Back in my truck, I sit for a moment, letting the engine idle. The airport's control tower is visible from here, a constant reminder piercing the skyline. Every time I see a private plane, my heart jumps. It's pathetic, really. I'm pathetic.

My phone buzzes, and for a split second, hope flares bright and sharp. But it's just Diego, sending me the week's schedule. I toss the phone onto the passenger seat

– the same seat where she sat, wearing my jacket because she was cold, her perfume lingering for days after.

Two weeks of silence. Two weeks of checking my phone, of crafting messages I never send, of wondering if I imagined the whole thing. *Was it just the storm? The isolation? Did I read too much into every touch, every smile, every whispered confession in the dark?*

I put the truck in drive, muscle memory guiding me through familiar streets. The snow is melting, revealing the town I've known all my life. Everything looks the same, but nothing feels right anymore. Not since she left.

I decide to head into town. Maybe being around people will help shake this fog that's settled over me.

Main Street still shows signs of the storm's aftermath. Piles of dirty snow line the sidewalks, though most of the roads are clear now. I wave to Mrs. Henderson sweeping her storefront and stop to help Mr. Patterson with a stubborn snowblower.

"You did good during that storm, Ben," Mr. Patterson says, clapping my shoulder. "Heard how you helped those stranded folks."

I force a smile. "Just doing what needed to be done."

The Bell & Whistle Café is warm and inviting, the smell of coffee and fresh pastries a temporary distraction. A new face greets me at the counter - young, pretty, with a bright smile that would have caught my attention a month ago.

"What can I get you?" She leans forward slightly, twirling her pen. "I'm Casey, by the way."

"Ben. Just coffee, black."

"You sure that's all? Our apple pie is amazing today." She winks, and I catch myself automatically smiling back, engaging in the familiar dance of casual flirtation.

I remember when this kind of attention used to give me a rush. The way Casey's leaning on the counter, that practiced tilt of her head - I know all the moves. Used to play this game myself, finding just the right words to make a pretty girl blush or laugh.

"You know what? The pie does sound good." I hear myself saying the words, going through the motions. Casey beams, but it doesn't stir anything in me. Not like the way Nora's subtle half-smile would make my heart race.

I settle into a corner booth, watching Casey float between tables with that deliberate sway to her hips. I'd have already figured out when her shift ended, maybe casually mentioned the live music at Murphy's tonight. The thrill of the chase, that's what Diego always called it.

My coffee arrives with an extra flourish, Casey's number scrawled on the napkin. Classic move. I used to live for these moments - the dance of flirtation, the possibilities wrapped up in seven digits.

"Let me know if you need anything else." She leans in closer than necessary, her perfume sweet and artificial. Nothing like Nora's clean, subtle scent.

"Thanks." I take a sip of coffee, remembering how Nora would cradle her cup in both hands, like she was soaking in its warmth. Everything comes back to her.

A group of girls enters the café, their laughter carrying across the room. The old Ben would have perked up, assessed the situation, maybe caught someone's eye. I was good at reading signals - a lingering glance, a nervous hair twist, the way they'd cluster together and whisper after I smiled. It was fun, harmless really. Most times it never went beyond playful banter, but I enjoyed the game itself.

The pie arrives, and Casey's hovering again. "So, are you from around here? I just moved up from Oregon last month."

Perfect opening. I know exactly how this script goes. Comment on the city, ask what brought her here, share a funny local story that makes me sound charming and down-to-earth. I've got a whole repertoire of these conversations.

"Born and raised," I say instead, keeping my eyes on my plate. "Thanks for the pie."

She lingers a moment longer, waiting for more, but I'm already lost in another memory - Nora telling me about her first solo flight, her eyes bright with passion, hands gesturing as she described the feeling of taking off alone for the first time.

The bell above the door chimes, and I glance up automatically. For a split second, every dark-haired woman makes my heart stop. But it's never her.

Casey makes another pass by my table, this time with a fresh pot of coffee. "Refill?"

"I'm good." I notice her nails - bright pink, perfectly manicured. Nora's were always short and practical, sometimes with traces of engine grease underneath despite her best efforts to keep them clean.

Two guys at the counter are obviously checking Casey out, and she's eating up the attention. I remember being like that - confident, carefree, always ready with a smooth line or winning smile. The guy I was before would have enjoyed this game, maybe even made it a challenge to get Casey's attention away from them.

Now it all seems so... empty. Like watching actors perform a play I used to know by heart but can't remember why I ever found it interesting.

My phone sits face-up on the table, silent as always. I check it anyway, swiping through old messages. The last one from Nora:

> Landing soon Talk later

That was two weeks ago. I've typed out dozens of messages since then, deleted them all.

Casey swings by one more time, her smile a little less bright now that I'm not playing along. "Anything else I can get you?"

"Just the check." I manage a polite smile, but it feels mechanical. I used to be better at this - making small talk, drawing people out, leaving them wanting more. It was second nature, as natural as breathing.

The old Ben would have already gotten her life story by now, maybe made plans for coffee or drinks. Would have enjoyed the simplicity of it - no complications, no real stakes, just the pure fun of making someone smile and feel special for a moment.

I leave cash on the table, enough for a decent tip. The napkin with Casey's number stays untouched. As I head for the door, I catch my reflection in the window - same face, same guy, but everything's different now.

"Hey, Huffman!" Old Joe calls from his usual corner booth. "You still fixing planes?"

I nod, grateful for the interruption. *He knows I do.* "Always."

"Got a pilot looking for a good mechanic. Their usual guy's out sick. Thought of you right away."

"Sure, I can take a look." Anything to keep busy. "Tell them to bring it by the hangar."

The familiar drive back to the hangar feels longer—each mile marked by memories.

The hangar doors are already open when I arrive. Strange, I could've sworn I closed them this morning. Did Diego leave them open?

My heart stops when I notice the Gulfstream.

A figure stands in the shadows.

I know that silhouette.

She steps into the light, and suddenly I can't breathe.

Nora.

Her uniform is crisp as ever, but there are shadows under her eyes that weren't there before. She looks tired, uncertain - beautiful.

"Ben."

One word. My name on her lips, and I'm moving before I can think. She meets me halfway, and when we collide, it's like every cliché I've ever rolled my eyes at.

Magnetic.

Inevitable.

Right.

My hands find her waist as hers grip my shoulders. "Where were you?" The words come out rougher than intended. "Two weeks, Nora. Not a word."

She pulls back just enough to meet my eyes. "I needed time. To think, to be sure." Her fingers trace my jaw, and I lean into the touch despite myself. "I went home, tried to convince myself that what happened here was just… circumstance. The storm, the isolation, the intensity of it all."

"And?"

"And I couldn't sleep. Couldn't focus. Kept reaching for my phone to tell you about my day, or thinking of your laugh, or remembering how you handled everything during the storm." She takes a shaky breath. "Then I realized something. Home isn't Seattle anymore. Home is where my heart is."

Her eyes lock with mine, vulnerable and sure all at once. "And somehow, without my permission, my heart decided to stay here. With you. I sold my house, closed my business—I want to open up something *here*—be with you, stay with you…I love you, Ben."

"And the Gulfstream? Did you steal that?" I ask, wondering.

Nora lets go a half-smile, "No silly, that's mine—just like you are."

The space between us disappears. Her body fits against mine like she never left—like these two weeks were just a bad dream. I can feel her heart racing, matching the wild rhythm of my own.

"God, I love you, Nora. So very, *very* much."

THE END

about trisha

Hey, it's Trish...

I'm a Romance Author of 40+ books, plus a Publishing House Owner of 50+ Pen Name Authors.

I've been writing romance with a whole lot of heat lately. I love to write fun, fast romances with witty leading ladies getting that gorgeous, sexy, yet lovable guy that doesn't take months to finish. Happily Ever After with a little bit of love angst in between. Whether you yearn for Historical or Modern, I always have a story for you!

Rejoice, Romance Reader...

For upcoming releases, book news, and other goodies, subscribe to my Newsletter!
https://bit.ly/49BR3UB

- instagram.com/authortrish
- amazon.com/Trisha-Fuentes/e/B002BME1MI
- facebook.com/booksbyTrish
- youtube.com/theardentartist

also by trisha fuentes

✻✻ Modern Romance ✻✻

A Sacrifice Play

Faded Dreams

Never Say Forever

* * *

✻✻ Historical ✻✻

The Anzan Heir

Magnet & Steele

The Relentless Rogue

One Starry Night

In The Moonlight With You

Captivating the Captain

The Merry Widow

Unrequited Love

The Summer Romance of the Duke

A Dare Maid in Vain

A Marriage of Mismatch

The Spoiled Duke

A Season of Second Chances

❋❋ Series ❋❋

HOLLINGER

Dare To Love - Book 1

A Matchless Match - Book 2

Arrogance & Conceit - Book 3

Impropriety - Book 4

SERVICE•DAUGHTER

The Steward's Daughter - Book 1

The Cook's Daughter - Book 2

The Curator's Daughter - Book 3

THUNDERBOLT

The Surprise Heir - Book 1

A Dance of Deception - Book 2

Win the Heart of a Duchess - Book 3

OBSESSION

Unsuitable Obsession - Part One

Broken Obsession - Part Two

ESCAPE

Swept Away - Book 1

Fire & Rescue - Book 2

The Domain King - Book 3

AGE•GAP•ROMANCE

Whispers of Yesterday - Book 1

His Encore, Her Ecstasy - Book 2

Against the Wind - Book 3

* * *

SERIAL•ROMANCE

The Rekindled Flame - Book 1

The Power of Two - Book 2

Facing the Past - Book 3

Taking a Chance - Book 4

Choosing the Future - Book 5

➥Full Paperback

https://bit.ly/3XbNK2e

www.ingramcontent.com/pod-product-compliance
Lightning Source LLC
LaVergne TN
LVHW021818060526
838201LV00058B/3435